S0-ARX-020

"Okay," Jarrod Said. "I'll Back Off.

How about dinner tomorrow night?"

Cassandra's eyebrows arched in faint amusement. "*That's* backing off?"

"Well, it all depends. You can consider it a business meeting. However, if you're more daring, consider it a real date."

Daring? No, she'd call it more like total insanity to accept his invitation when the man aroused her senses so thoroughly. Still, it would present a good opportunity to discuss her new horse. At least, that was what she told herself right before she agreed.

"Tomorrow night will be fine. I'll make dinner for us here."

His arm went around her shoulder and squeezed it playfully. "Just what I love. A cheap date."

"Ah, but I haven't said if this was business or pleasure, have I?"

Jarrod opened the door of his truck and sat down inside. "Call it whatever you want, Cassie. The pleasure's all mine either way."

Dear Reader:

Sensuous, emotional, compelling...these are all words that describe Silhouette Desire. If this is your first Desire novel, let me extend an invitation for you to revel in the pleasure of a tantalizing, fulfilling love story. If you're a regular reader, you already know that you're in for a treat!

A Silhouette Desire can encompass many varying moods and tones. The story can be deeply moving and dramatic, or charming and lighthearted. But no matter what, each and every Silhouette Desire is a terrific romance written by and for today's woman.

April is a special month here at Silhouette Desire. First, there's *Warrior,* one of Elizabeth Lowell's books in the *Western Lovers* series. And don't miss *The Drifter* by Joyce Thies, April's *Man of the Month,* which is sure to delight you.

Paula Detmer Riggs makes her Silhouette Desire debut with *Rough Passage,* an exciting story of trust and love. Rounding out April are wonderful stories by Laura Leone, Donna Carlisle and Jessica Barkley. There's something for everyone, every mood, every taste.

So give in to Desire...you'll be glad you did.

All the best,

Lucia Macro
Senior Editor

JESSICA
BARKLEY

FRAME-UP

SILHOUETTE *Desire*®

Published by Silhouette Books New York

America's Publisher of Contemporary Romance

SILHOUETTE BOOKS
300 East 42nd St., New York, N.Y. 10017

FRAME-UP

Copyright © 1991 by Cori L. Deyoe

All rights reserved. Except for use in any review,
the reproduction or utilization of this work in
whole or in part in any form by any electronic,
mechanical or other means, now known or
hereafter invented, including xerography,
photocopying and recording, or in any information
storage or retrieval system, is forbidden without
the permission of Silhouette Books, 300 E. 42nd St.,
New York, N.Y. 10017

ISBN: 0-373-05635-4

First Silhouette Books printing April 1991

All the characters in this book are fictitious. Any
resemblance to actual persons, living or dead, is
purely coincidental.

® and ™: Trademarks used with authorization.
Trademarks indicated with ® are registered
in the United Patent and Trademark Office,
the Canada Trade Mark Office and in
other countries.

Printed in the U.S.A.

Books by Jessica Barkley

Silhouette Special Edition

Into the Sunset #406

Silhouette Desire

Montana Man #556
Frame-Up #635

JESSICA BARKLEY

shares her life in Wisconsin with her husband, their daughter, two dogs, fourteen cats and five horses. A born city-girl who turned country, she enjoys working in her garden, competing in distance rides and photographing nature. Her favorite time, however, is spent spinning romance tales on her word processor, while Jetae and Tasha sleep curled up in the doorway of her den.

To Linda, a true and lifelong friend,
whether we work together or not;
and to Ann, who always let me sit
in the front seat

One

Jarrod Fitzgerald stared at the phone message in his hand for a long moment as a thoughtful frown creased his forehead. It had been at least six months since he'd last spoken to the man whose name was scrawled on the pink pad. He shook off the old premonition that something was amiss as he slowly picked up the receiver and dialed the number.

"Hello?"

"Hi, Les. It's Jarrod."

"Jarrod!" Les Adams exclaimed in obvious relief. "Thanks for returning my call. I was hoping you'd be able to get back to me soon."

"How's that lovely wife of yours?"

"Anxious for me to finally retire."

Jarrod shook his head as he solemnly toyed with the phone cord. "So the rumors I've heard are true? You're actually going to stop practicing?"

"After forty years of being a vet, I suppose it's time. Which brings me to the reason I called. I have a favor to ask of you, Jarrod. Actually, it's more than a favor. It's something that would mean a great deal to me, not to mention how much it would mean to a close friend of mine."

Ordinarily he would have agreed without even asking. This time, Jarrod hesitated. "What's the favor?"

"As I said, I'm retiring at the end of this month. I know how busy you are, so I've secured various other vets to take over all of my clients except one. It's a very special account, and I was hoping I could talk you into taking it over for me."

Equal amounts of suspicion and curiosity surged through him. "So, who's the client?"

"Cassie Malone."

Cassie Malone. If he'd had the time to think about it, Jarrod would have guessed as much. "Why won't anyone else take over her account?" he asked, even though he knew perfectly well why.

"You see, Jarrod, that's the thing. Cassie needs a special vet to treat her horses—"

"Special as in one who'll work for nothing?" Jarrod cut in bluntly.

"No, not exactly. She pays me for medicine and supplies and such. But I consider what she does to be such a worthy cause, I've never charged her for my time." Les paused. "Do you know her?"

"You know damn well I know her, Les."

"Yes, well, then you know what a wonderful thing it is she's doing with those horses. All the money she takes in goes right back into her farm, and I've always felt good about being able to help her out by donating my services. She went through quite a rough time a few years ago, with her father and everything. You remember Mike Malone, don't you?"

"Yeah," Jarrod muttered. "I sure do."

"So what do you say? Will you take over Cassie's account for me?"

Jarrod let the receiver slip away from his ear as distant, nagging memories flooded his mind. Images appeared, images of a once-respected horseman, ruined by scandal, who then turned to a bottle as his only companion. Images of the man's daughter, fiercely devoted throughout the whole ordeal, who was forced to change her entire life-style due to her father's carelessness. And then there were the images of himself, with his own harsh accusations...

"Jarrod? Are you still there?"

Jarrod slowly put the receiver back up to his ear. "I'm here."

"Do you want me to give you some time to think about it?"

"No, that won't be necessary." A rueful smile formed on his lips. "I'll do it."

"What do you think?" Cassie asked, unable to keep the anxiousness out of her voice.

Les Adams straightened up in careful stages. One hand went automatically to his lower back to massage the muscles there while the other hand patted the underweight mare's neck. He turned and smiled reassuringly at Cassie. "She's coming along just fine. That bowed tendon went too long without treatment to heal up one hundred percent, but you've done wonders with it since you've had her. She'll probably have a touch of a limp on that leg the rest of her life, though."

Cassie reached up and fondly stroked the mare's nose. "That doesn't matter, as long as she can get around all right and isn't in pain."

"You're not going to adopt this one back out, are you?"

She shrugged one shoulder casually, but she knew Les wouldn't be fooled by the gesture. "I don't know. It all depends on how well her tendon holds up, I guess. Now that it's stronger, I'll be able to get some weight back on her. No one would adopt her looking like this anyway."

"You can't keep every horse you get in here," Les reminded her gently. "You can barely afford to provide for the ones you have now."

Cassie sighed. "I'll manage, Les. I always do." She put the gentle mare back into her box stall and latched the door. She paused for a moment outside the stall, her eyes skimming over the emaciated horse. Her grip tightened on the lead rope in her hand as a renewed sense of rage filled her. This mare had one of the most easygoing, sweetest personalities of any she'd had in her barns in a long time. How could anyone have treated her so badly? Then as the horse gave her arm a friendly nudge over the stall door, Cassie's anger dissolved away into tenderness for the animal. Les had seen through her again. She knew she'd never let this one go. The mare was too special.

But then, there weren't many horses she'd come across since she'd started this that hadn't been. She'd been working with a county humane organization for two years now, taking in horses they removed from abusive or neglectful owners. Her job was to heal them, physically as well as mentally, feed them back up to their normal weight, and retrain any that had developed nasty habits as a result of their previous handling. Once that was done, which sometimes took months, she adopted them back out to carefully screened homes.

It was a job she'd volunteered for, and she wasn't paid by the organization or anyone else for her work. When she sold a reformed horse, more often than not the money she received turned out to be only a fraction of the amount she'd spent on its care. But it didn't matter, for she loved what she did. It was just that some horses were easier than others for her to let go of when the time came. And this particular mare was one of far too many that she simply couldn't part with.

She walked over and hung the lead rope on a vacant hook near the tack room, smiling at Les along the way. "Want to come in for a cup of coffee?"

"Sure. There's something I need to talk to you about anyway."

Cassie's eyes darted quickly to his face, but he avoided meeting her gaze. The twinge of uneasiness his words had brought her was replaced by a strong foreboding of dread as she saw the tight set of his mouth. She'd known Les Adams a long time, and she could read him as well as he could her. What he had to tell her couldn't be good.

It took quite a bit of concentration to keep her hands steady as she poured them both a cup of lukewarm, hours-old coffee. She sat down at the kitchen table then and simply waited.

Les fingered the handle of the ceramic mug for several minutes. "Cassie," he said reluctantly at last, "I don't know how else to say this except to come right out with it. I'm retiring at the end of the month."

"You're what?" she squeaked.

"I'm sorry I waited so long to let you know. Of all my clients, I knew you'd be the hardest one to tell. I didn't want to leave you in a bind, so I waited to give you the news until I had another vet lined up to take over here for me."

"Another vet?" she repeated numbly. "But I don't want another vet!" Les had been so good to her over the last two years. His unending patience and sensitive demeanor always had a calming effect on her horses. On the awful occasions when a horse had been beyond saving, Les had offered her compassion and a shoulder to cry on. She couldn't imagine entrusting her horses to anyone else.

"Everything will be just fine, you'll see. The vet I got for you—"

"But couldn't you just keep on doing my horses?" she interrupted desperately, hating herself for even asking. "You don't live that far from here, and it wouldn't take much of your time. I'd pay you whatever I could..." As Les slowly shook his head, the words died off in her throat and her heart sank still further.

"I'm sorry, Cassie. I'd be happy to do that for a while if I could, but my wife has always had her heart set on retiring in Florida. We bought a condo down there, and we're moving the first of next month. I won't be around here anymore."

Cassie closed her eyes briefly while she digested the awful news. She really had no right to feel so selfishly miserable for herself. Les deserved a comfortable retirement, and she should be happy for him. But it was a double blow to lose him as a vet and a friend. She'd probably never see him again, and that was very hard to think about.

"So who did you get to take over for you?" she asked weakly.

Les faltered for a fraction of a second. "One of the vets at the Bluegrass Equine Clinic."

Warning bells rang inside her, but Cassie was still too stunned over Les's news to figure out why. "He'll never be as good as you," she told him solemnly.

"You just might be surprised about that."

Cassie simultaneously raised her coffee cup and pushed all thoughts of a new vet out of her mind. "Here's to you, Les," she said with a lot more cheeriness than she really felt. "I can't thank you enough for all you've done for me. I'll be miserable trying to get along around here without you, but I'm just thankful I got the chance to know you at all. I hope you have a wonderful life in Florida."

And may your replacement be one-tenth the man you are, she added silently.

She knew the horse was going to be a problem the moment she laid eyes on him. The way he kicked impatiently at the back of the trailer when it pulled up to her barn gave her the first clue, and the way he burst out of it once the ramp was lowered gave her another. But it was the look in his eyes that gave him completely away. The fierce hatred and stubborn pride that burned so clearly in his large brown eyes was intense enough to send a shiver up her spine. One look at his battered and bony body told her this horse had been to hell and back. Most horses would have simply given up after such treatment and have a dull, listless, apathetic look to them. But not this one. He had learned to survive human injustice a different way. He was fighting mad.

Cassie's gaze scanned the horse quickly as Stacey, the representative from the humane organization, walked him around. His black coat had no shine to it whatsoever and a combination of dried mud and manure was caked on his belly and legs. His hooves obviously hadn't been trimmed in months and were so long that they'd flattened out and curled up slightly on the ends. She could count every bone in his body. He had several fresh wounds, as well as long, thin scars on his chest and rump that had most likely been caused by a whip.

She continued to watch the horse move around for another few minutes, marveling that he had the strength to take a single step, let alone toss his head rebelliously and try to pull away from the small woman who held him tightly in check. It was while the horse was skirting around in a circle that she caught a glimpse between his back legs.

"Stacey, this horse is a stallion!"

The look Stacey gave her was mixed with chagrin and guilt. "I know. We were afraid if we told you he wasn't a gelding, you wouldn't take him. And you know if you don't, he'll have to be put down. There's no one else we can possibly leave him with except you."

Cassie shook her head and cursed under her breath. She'd known Stacey ever since she'd started her volunteer work with the humane group, and the other woman knew exactly how to get to her. She'd never taken on a stallion before and she had no real desire to do so now. Especially this one. It was tough enough trying to rehabilitate a mare or gelding who had become a rogue, but a stallion was something altogether different. It would take an awful lot of her time, and that was one thing she had precious little of as it was.

She was seriously thinking of refusing and begging for them to find someone else, anyone else, when the horse abruptly stopped his restless movements and simply stood there, watching her. A chill went through her as she met his steady gaze. What had made the stallion suddenly decide to give her his undivided attention? she wondered. She hadn't moved since he'd been unloaded from the trailer, and before this instant he had steadfastly ignored her. It was almost as if he'd read her mind, and was now sending her a silent challenge.

Cassie forced herself to relax and release the breath she hadn't even been aware she'd been holding. A small smile played on her lips as she berated herself for so blatantly anthropomorphizing. She'd been accused and criticized countless times in her life for thinking of her animals in human terms. Still, this time she couldn't help herself. Something had passed between horse and human in that one moment, and in some inexplicable way she felt bonded to the animal. There was no way she could send him away now. Especially when the only alternative for him was death.

"I'll take him, Stacey. I'll probably be sorry, but I'll take him."

Stacey grinned. "Thanks, Cassie." She led the horse over to his new caretaker. "He looks like he might've been something at one time."

As Cassie reached to take the lead rope, the stallion pinned back his ears and swung out his head to bite her arm. She'd noticed him trying similar antics while Stacey was holding him, so she'd been on the alert. Instinctively she raised up her elbow and caught him in the nose, thereby thwarting his attack. "Yeah, I'll bet he was something sometime," she commented. "The question is, what?"

"That's for you to find out. I've really got to run now. I'll talk to you later."

"Sure, if this guy doesn't kill me first," Cassie said grimly as the horse made another attempt to nip her. She jerked firmly on the lead rope to hold him off. If he'd simply been a spoiled horse with a bad habit, she'd have done more to discipline him. But now was not the time for that.

"Good luck," Stacey called as she hopped into her truck. A moment later, truck and trailer were out of sight. Only a thin cloud of dust remained behind.

"Luck!" Cassie echoed doubtfully to the horse at her side. "I think I'm going to need more than that with you, big fella."

The stallion tossed his head as if in agreement.

Twenty minutes later, Cassie was on the phone to the Bluegrass Equine Clinic. It wasn't until she'd started speaking to the secretary that she realized she'd never found out the name of the vet Les had secured for her. The secretary told her she'd check on it and send the vet out as soon as possible.

If only Les hadn't already retired and left for Florida, Cassie thought glumly as she hung up the phone. He'd been gone a week now, and she considered herself quite fortunate to have gotten by that long without needing a vet. What she wouldn't give to have Les's soothing manner around today. This horse was hardly the one who should be an unknown vet's first patient on her farm. But since the stallion had to be checked over and vaccinated, she really had no choice.

Cassie grabbed an apple to munch on as she wandered back out to the barn. She'd put the big horse in her largest box stall to relax and get his bearings, but he hadn't settled down one bit. He could smell the other horses in the barn, and between that and being in a new place, he was very restless.

She spoke quietly to him, using nonsense words in a calming way. The horse cocked one ear in her direction before both ears flattened against his head. He kept his distance at the back of the stall and just stared defiantly at her.

After finishing off the best parts of the apple, she slipped inside the stall and offered him the core in her hand. She was met with open hostility, but at least the horse didn't charge her. A few minutes later, she sensed rather than overtly noticed his slight shift in attitude for the better, perhaps caused by the fragrant, tempting apple core she still held in her hand.

The stallion took one cautious step toward her, and she praised him lavishly. Just as he started to advance one more foot, he suddenly snorted and shook his head furiously. He pawed the straw with one overgrown hoof for a few seconds, then danced nervously around, shifting from his front feet to his back feet as if he wanted to bolt. His ears were flattened back so tightly against his head, she couldn't even see them.

"Easy, boy," she crooned. The horse was ready to explode and she was unsure of the best way to deal with it. *Idiot!* she chided herself. She knew better than to have put herself in this position so quickly after getting the horse. It was too soon to force him to call his bluff or back off. Yet, for a short time when he'd taken that first tentative step toward her, she'd actually thought he was softening a bit. But now—

The next few seconds passed by in a blur. The stallion reared and struck out at the same time she heard the stall door sliding open. The next thing she knew, she was being yanked forcibly out of the stall and then released so quickly that she found herself stumbling to regain her balance.

"What the—" she sputtered, but the rest of her choice comment was stuck in her throat as the tall man in front of her slammed the stall door shut and latched it before turning around.

She had no idea how long she simply stood there, staring at him in utter disbelief. Jarrod Fitzgerald, here on her farm? It was inconceivable. Fury rumbled in her like a brewing thunderstorm.

"What the hell are you doing here?" she demanded.

Jarrod hadn't expected a jovial greeting, so he was far from surprised at her outrage. His own ire had been piqued the moment he'd seen her in the stall with that black beast. "What in the hell were you doing in *there?*" he countered, jerking his head toward the stallion.

"I don't see where that's any of your business." Her hands on her hips, she continued to glare at him. "You didn't answer my question."

Jarrod's eyes narrowed slightly. "I figured you would tell me why I was here."

"What are you talking about?"

"Les didn't tell you?"

"Tell me what?" Then she let out a short, mirthless laugh as realization sank in. "You've got to be kidding."

"Kidding?"

"*You're* Les's replacement?"

"You're lucky I was in the neighborhood when your call came in. If I hadn't shown up when I did, that rogue could've killed you. I hope you're not always so reckless."

"I was doing just fine with him until you showed up!" she snapped defensively. "I wondered why he went berserk so unexpectedly."

"He went berserk because he's a dangerous brute. Look at him! Even now he's outraged he can't get at us."

Cassie glanced over at the horse and saw he was pacing rapidly around the small confines of the stall, his ears still pinned angrily. After every few steps, he struck out with a back hoof at the wooden planks that made up the walls. "He's upset he can't get at you, you mean. He has no reason to want to hurt me."

"And he does me? Give me a break, lady. I suppose the next thing you're going to tell me is that he only reared up in there because he was trying to get at me in order to protect you!"

"Of course not. I'm hardly that ignorant."

"You must be to risk being in the same stall with that killer."

"I only got him an hour ago," she informed him tartly. "He needs time to get used to me and his new surroundings and then he'll be fine."

"I've seen plenty of horses like him before. When they get to this stage, they're no good for anything. He should be put down."

Cassie shook her head. "You must know your opinion means absolutely nothing to me. Now get off my farm."

"I think you should reconsider that statement," he said calmly. "Who else would you get to treat your horses? Les asked damn near every vet in the area, and no one would do it without charging you for the calls and diagnoses except me."

"I'd rather pay the most expensive vet in Kentucky than have you ever lay a finger on one of my horses."

Jarrod smothered back a sigh of frustration. He'd known she was going to give him a hard time, although he had hoped Les would've smoothed things over for him before retiring. Studying Cassie now, he couldn't help but get caught up in her beauty, exemplified now because she was all riled up and spitting fire. Her long, thick dark hair was so black he swore the highlights that shone off of it were a deep blue. But maybe that was just an illusion, caused by the reflection from a pair of the bluest eyes he'd ever seen. Those eyes were shooting off angry sparks at him now.

He had no doubt Cassie's wrath would make most men back off. Not him. He was completely intrigued. It was as if he'd stepped back in time, and although it had been years since he'd spoken to her, he'd never really gotten over this fascination. With an inward grimace, he realized if he didn't handle this exactly right, it would probably be a few more years before he had another chance.

"The past is best forgotten, Cassie," he suggested softly.

"The past is never forgotten." She turned her back on him and faced the fretting stallion. "Or forgiven."

"Listen, I could say I'm sorry for what happened to your father, and it would be the honest truth, but that isn't going to change the past. All I can tell you is I'd like to take over being your vet.''

She whirled around defiantly. "I don't need your pity.''

"I wouldn't think of offering you any.'' A steady smile built up fraction by fraction on his lips. "I'm a good vet, and my services are cheap. I think your horses are more important to you than your pride. So, what can I do for you today?''

Cassie opened her mouth, but her intended response was quickly lost. How long had it been since she'd witnessed his considerable charm? Evidently not long enough, for she was no more immune to it now than she had been before.

She'd conveniently forgotten how stunningly handsome he was. Her eyes were drawn immediately to the dimples that highlighted his cheeks, and from there traveled down to the slight cleft in his chiseled chin. Her attention dipped to focus on his rangy, muscular body. She'd rarely seen a man whose physique was complemented by functional clothing, but Jarrod's coveralls appeared to have been tailor-made to fit him perfectly in all the right places. The man should be in an ad for cologne or something, she thought with a touch of irritation.

Her gaze rested momentarily on his disarming smile, a smile so fetching she could only guess at how many hearts it had broken over the years. With some difficulty, she forced her expression to transform from appreciative to remote.

"You're right about one thing,'' she told him. "My horses are very important to me. That's why I'm not about to have that stallion put down. If that's the kind of attitude you'd have about all my difficult horses, there's no point in discussing this any further.''

"Okay, I'll admit I might have reacted a little hastily about that. It won't happen again.'' He nodded at the stallion and fought to keep his voice casual. "What's the story on him, anyway?''

"Almost every horse I take in here is either the victim of neglect or else the victim of abuse. That big guy hit the jackpot," she said sarcastically. "He was the victim of both."

"He looks Thoroughbred. Did he race?"

"I don't know. The man he was taken from has a small-time racing stable, but, as often seems to be the case, this was the only horse in bad enough shape to be confiscated. How some people can decide to mistreat a single animal out of thirty is beyond me. The owner sure wasn't very eager to give us any information about him."

"The bastard obviously couldn't handle him, even though he tried to with a whip. So I guess he just let him sit in a stall and rot, huh?"

Cassie nodded. "He's certainly not the first fool to think he could starve a horse into submission. With a few, though, like this horse, it backfires."

"And then you take over, mend their bodies and minds, and turn them into useful creatures again."

She glanced sharply at him, certain he was being contemptuous. What she saw instead was a look of genuine respect on his face. "That's the idea."

Jarrod strode nonchalantly over to another box stall. "So tell me about this one. He looks like he's already been re-formed."

She had to laugh. "He should. I raised that one from a foal. He was never abused; in fact, quite the opposite. I spoil him too much, but he's a gentleman and doesn't take advantage of it."

"Oh." He moved on to the next stall. "Well, what about this one?"

"Look, I'm not sure what the point of all this is, and I really have a lot to do today. So, if you don't mind . . ."

"I get the hint." Jarrod headed toward his truck, and was surprised when she followed. "Can I come back tomorrow and see that stallion?"

She looked away from his earnest gray eyes, eyes that could still penetrate one minute and caress the next. "I don't think that would be a good idea," she said at last.

"Why not?"

"My horses need special care and understanding. I don't think you're the right man for the job."

"Can you afford anyone else at full price?"

She couldn't even afford to eat a good steak dinner more than once a month, but she wouldn't tell him that. Her horses came first, and they always had. "No, I can't," she acknowledged.

"Then give me a chance."

"I guess I could." Cassie heard the words, but she couldn't believe they came out of her mouth. She was sure she'd been about to refuse him again.

"Good. I'll see you tomorrow, then."

"All right, but only to look at some of my other horses. I don't want you near my stallion."

"I might give you the same advice."

"You might. But I wouldn't take it."

"And it doesn't make sense for me to take yours. I saw a few open cuts on him that have to be taken care of, and he should have a tetanus shot. He needs looking at long before I might win over your trust."

"That may be true, but we'll just have to take things one day at a time."

Jarrod got into his truck and rolled down the window. "Just do me a favor and stay out of that stallion's reach when you're here alone."

"That happens to be most of the time, Doctor. You worry about your job and I'll worry about mine."

He held up both hands for a moment before starting the engine. With a shrug and a wave, he drove away.

As Cassie watched him disappear down the driveway, it occurred to her that she hadn't felt this unsettled for a very long time. What in the world had she gotten herself into?

Two

Cassie walked slowly back to the stallion's stall after Jarrod left. A light layer of sweat now covered the still-agitated horse's coat, giving it a shine that would disappear once again when he was dry. She'd always had the gift of looking at a horse when it was in less-than-prime condition and seeing a clear picture in her mind of that same horse filled out and healthy. Many horses other people wouldn't give a second look at were given another chance in life because Cassie had the insight to see those horses as they could be, and not as they were when she first saw them.

Looking carefully at the stallion in front of her now, her brain started ticking away. By adding pounds here, rounding out there, trimming up the scruffy hair, and restoring a healthy glow to his coat, she figured she had the makings of a first-class horse. Then her eyes widened suddenly as she imagined the stallion in top form. He looked vaguely familiar, she thought with a stir of uneasiness. Her sharp gaze went over him again, noting the dirty white star on his fore-

head and what appeared to be one white stocking underneath a coating of manure on his right rear leg.

She closed her eyes and willed the picture of the stallion
to come in clearer in her mind. He definitely reminded her
of another horse, a Thoroughbred, but which one? She
shook her head impatiently. It was like trying to search for
something amid dense fog—the harder you looked, the
fuzzier the picture got. She felt the same frustration now,
knowing deep down there was another horse in her memory that was nearly identical to the black stallion presently
in her barn, but still unable to quite put her finger on the
identity of the other horse.

"Well, big guy," she said to the horse with quiet resolve,
"I guess I'm just going to have to do a little digging around
into your past. In the meantime, you're going to need a
name. The creep who owned you wouldn't tell anyone what
he called you. Not that you'd probably want to be reminded of anything that had to do with him anyway, but it
might've been nice to know."

Cassie moved closer to the stall, and the horse immediately backed farther into the corner. She leaned forward
until her face rested against the cool steel bars on the front
of the door and sighed.

Although picking out a name for an animal had to be one
of the things she was absolutely worst at, she'd known the
minute she'd seen this horse what she wanted to call him.
She'd dreamed of having a black horse ever since she was a
little girl, and she'd had the name chosen the whole time.
But she was an adult now, and the name hardly seemed like
something a mature person would think up.

"Oh, why not? Your new name," she proclaimed, smiling in spite of herself, "is Midnight. I hope you like it."
Then she became solemn again, and a pensive frown replaced the silly grin. "Now if only I could figure out the
name of the horse you're a dead ringer for, I'd be all set."

As she left the barn and headed for the house, she realized what a blessing it was to have the puzzle about the horse

to keep her brain occupied. Without that mystery badger-
ing at her, her mind would most certainly be on a certain
handsome two-legged animal instead of a four-legged one.
It was rather ironic that both had disrupted her life on the
same day. And she couldn't trust either one of them.

Once inside the house, Cassie paused at the door to her
den. She glanced in at the mahogany desk that sat so re-
gally by the window, its top covered with paperwork and
bills that needed her attention. She kept on walking. Not in
the mood to face the verity of her financial situation, Cassie went into the kitchen instead.

As she poured herself a cup of coffee, a bittersweet smile
touched her lips. When was she ever in the mood to go over
her bills? Cassie sank down heavily into a chair and for a
brief moment allowed herself the luxury of imagining she
was filthy rich and didn't need to bow to Jarrod Fitzgerald
to treat her horses. She still found it hard to believe he'd
agreed to take over her account without charging the full
amount for his services. What was he after? There had to be
something in it for him, and she fervently wished she knew
what it was. If he showed up tomorrow, she was going to
come right out and ask him.

Cassie set her coffee cup down with a thud that echoed
loudly on the wooden table. She half hoped Jarrod wouldn't
come back, special rate or no special rate. She'd gotten by
perfectly well these last few years without charity from
anyone, and she could keep on doing just that if she had to.
But then reality forced its way unwillingly into her pondering, and she had no choice but to accept the fact that she
needed every spare dime she had for feed, medicine, sup-
plements, and maintenance. If only her father had left her
a little more money...

She cut off that line of thinking by taking a big gulp of
coffee. Such fanciful reveries were nothing but a waste of
time. She was grateful her father had willed her enough to
buy this small farm, yet she couldn't help but feel a trace of
resentment along with it. If her father hadn't been set up

and ruined, he wouldn't have drank away so much of his money in the final months of his life in an effort to forget the past.

In one determined swig, Cassie drained the rest of her coffee. That was another mystery she'd vowed long ago to clear up someday. How, she had no idea. But it wasn't right that people should remember her father, who'd been such a magnificent horseman, as a careless, irresponsible bum. She knew much of that stigma had been passed on to her after his death, as grossly unfair as it was. That was one reason she'd gone into rehabilitating needy horses; despite a lifetime of experience with racehorses, she couldn't get a decent job at a respectable stable simply because she was Michael Malone's daughter.

Cassie scorned the whole blasted bunch of them now, all the rich Thoroughbred owners who looked down their noses at her. It had taken her a while, but she no longer felt inferior to them. She had as much pride as they had money, even if she did have to swallow it once in a while. Like with Jarrod. She found it especially hard to bite down her pride where he was concerned, because he'd been one of those who had openly accused her father of negligence. The injustice of it all still festered in her like an open wound.

Being near Jarrod again had stirred up more emotions than simple anger about her father. It was as if time and tragedy had never gotten in the way. They'd never spoken more than a dozen words to each other back then, but his smile still made her knees a little wobbly, his gray eyes still seemed to burn a path straight to her soul. It made her as uncomfortable now as it did all those years ago. She must have been out of her mind to agree to let him **int**o her life, even on such a limited basis.

Cassie pushed aside her misgivings about Jarrod while she rinsed out her cup. Maybe he wouldn't even show up tomorrow, and then she wouldn't have to worry about it. She hadn't been the most gracious person in the world toward him. Maybe he'd decide it wasn't worth his trouble to put up with the hassles he'd get from her. Maybe she'd never see him again.

Strangely enough, the thought of that left her even more disconcerted.

Jarrod slowed down his truck and turned on the right directional light. When his vehicle was even with the mailbox that read Malone, he came to a complete stop and shifted into neutral. Almost twenty-four hours had passed since he'd been in this exact spot, and he still wasn't completely sure he wanted to take that final, irreversible step of pulling into her driveway. He had the unnerving feeling that if he did so, no matter how hard he might fight it, a part of his life would change forever.

But he had some things to make up to her, things that had plagued him for a long time. Both of their lives might have turned out so differently if only Ebony Fire hadn't died. And the great racehorse wouldn't have, if Mike Malone had been more conscientious in his job.

His thoughts took a trip into the past, and it was a far from pleasant journey. What a shock it had been for him three years ago to return from a week-long conference to find his most famous patient dead. Horse of the Year as a two-year-old, Ebony Fire had the brightest possible future before him. Sure, any little thing could always go wrong where a horse was concerned, but the fact that the racehorse's life had been lost due to the careless feeding of moldy hay—well, it had been especially hard to accept. Perhaps doubly so because he hadn't been there when it happened.

The shock of it all had brought out some very angry, harsh words on his part against Mike Malone, Ebony Fire's caretaker. Maybe, if he had to do it over again, he'd soften the accusations just a bit. Not that he doubted Malone's guilt, but he'd never felt good about what had happened to Cassie as a result of her father getting fired. He knew she'd steadfastly refused to believe in her father being at fault, and judging by her reaction when she saw him yesterday, she still harbored some ill feelings. Had she ever felt anything else?

Jarrod hardly considered himself a so-called ladies' man, but he'd never been one who lacked for female attention, either. Yet from the first day he'd seen Cassie, she'd skittered away, barely giving him notice. He'd been attracted to her immediately, but it had certainly seemed to be one-sided. It had confused him as much as it had tantalized him. But before he'd made any progress with her, Ebony Fire had died. And that, most certainly, had been the end of that.

Taking a deep breath, Jarrod shifted the truck into gear and started up the gravel drive. He owed her something, and if the only way to repay his debt to her was by being a cheap vet, then so be it. He could live with that, and it was a good excuse to get close to her as well.

Cassie appeared from inside the barn just as Jarrod got out of his truck. If anything, she looked more beautiful than she had yesterday, he thought with a stir of restlessness. The bright noon sun shone down on her black hair, creating glimmering rays of deep violet streaks amid the waves. A slightly upturned nose and makeup-free face perhaps took her out of the classically gorgeous bracket, but nonetheless her features couldn't have been any more alluring. Her casual stance as she leaned against the barn door accentuated long slender limbs that were further enriched by the close fit of her worn jeans. She wore a light blue T-shirt that was neither too tight nor too loose, but simply molded itself to her gently rounded breasts.

His gaze traveled all the way down to her feet, and he smiled to himself when he noticed her wearing scuffed-up white tennies. He couldn't think of another woman he knew who didn't wear the traditional and fashionable cowboy boots around her horses.

"You're still in one piece," he observed. "Did you take my advice after all and stay away from that stallion?"

"Don't start with me," she warned flatly.

He slipped her a grin. "Whatever you say. So, do I get the honor of treating some of your horses today, or did I waste my time coming out here?"

She shrugged in an effort to appear indifferent. "It's up to you."

Jarrod shoved his hands into the pockets of his coveralls in sudden annoyance. "Oh, like you're doing me some giant favor by letting me around your precious horses? I've got news for you, Cassie. I happen to treat some of the most expensive and valuable Thoroughbred racehorses in the state of Kentucky."

"I know perfectly well the kind of horses you minister to," she shot back, "as well as the kind of people who own them. Those horses are commodities, nothing more. They're money-making machines that are treated with care as long as they keep winning. As soon as they're not, this is what happens to them." Her arm made a wide, sweeping gesture that encompassed her farm.

"You're quite the little cynic, aren't you? That's kind of funny considering you and your father both worked at some of those money-hungry racehorse stables, including Nathan Hall's."

"My father was the most sensitive, compassionate, and caring man I've ever known, and he had an incredible way with horses. He was nothing like that pig of a man we worked for."

"That's no way to talk about your neighbor."

"Who also happens to be one of your clients."

"So? Nate might not be the most merciful horseman in the world, but he never got careless and killed a horse, either."

"My father didn't have a thing to do with that horse's death," she said slowly and distinctly, but her voice was barely more than a raspy whisper. "He was framed or he was someone's convenient fall guy, but he was not the one responsible for Ebony Fire dying."

One corner of Jarrod's heart softened at her tortured expression. However, her belief in her father's innocence wasn't enough to make him do the same. "Maybe," he conceded. "I guess no one will ever really know that for sure now, will they?"

She shook her head. "*I* know, and that's all that matters." But it wasn't, not really. She would've given anything to have been able to clear her father's name while he was still alive, more so to assuage his own shattered self-image than to forgo the repercussions the incident had caused in her own life. But since his death, she'd had to gradually release the bitterness that burned in her, and simply go on. It was at odd, unexpected moments like this that she was ruefully reminded just how much it still hurt, even after all this time. The fire inside her might have been reduced from a big blaze to a controlled smolder, but it remained nonetheless.

"I'm sorry, Cassie," Jarrod murmured. "I shouldn't have brought that up about your father. I hardly knew him, but he did have an impressive reputation before, well, you know. It's a shame a man's whole lifetime career can be forever tarnished by one incident."

At his sudden show of tender sympathy, Cassie's indignation eased away. "Thanks," she told him somewhat warily.

Jarrod offered her a quizzical smile. "I think I better ask you one more time. Are you going to let me treat your horses?"

His voice was as soft and smooth as a feather, and it floated over her like a tender caress. She closed her eyes briefly against the flutter of tingling sensations she felt as her body immediately responded. She was more than a little shocked that she could go so abruptly from nearly hating him to almost wanting him.

Wanting him? At that astounding thought, her eyes flew open and she pursed her lips with grim resolution. She couldn't help it if the man could charm the socks off her when he tried, but she could make sure she took it at face value and didn't let it carry her any further than mild fascination. There were her horses to think of, and with their welfare at stake, she could overcome almost anything.

She returned his questioning smile with a guarded one of her own. "I'll probably live to regret it, but yes, I'll give you a try."

"Then I better get started. I've got quite a full afternoon ahead of me."

Switching into her best detached, businesslike attitude, Cassie turned and led the way to the mare with the bowed tendon. "I'd like you to look at her leg. I had Les check it right before he retired, and he said it was about as good as it was going to get." She paused while leading the mare out of the box stall. "I've been feeding and exercising her more since then, and I'd just like to make sure the leg is holding up all right."

Jarrod observed the leg in question critically from all angles before bending down and running his fingers over the tendon. He checked it for soreness and filling, then flexed the joint. After treating countless racehorses over the years with the same type of injury, he was right at home examining this mare.

"Walk her down the length of the aisle, then trot her straight back at me," he instructed. Cassie did as he asked, and when she stopped back in front of him, he smiled. "I agree with Les in that the tendon is as far healed as it will ever be. She favors it very slightly when she trots, but there's no pain in it. If you build up her conditioning slowly, she'll probably be a decent pleasure horse. Just be careful she never gets too fat. The less strain on that leg, the better. Next?"

"Well, there's this other mare down here I've had for three months now. She's been wormed and her teeth have been checked, but I can't seem to put any weight on her. She gets exercised lightly every day, although you wouldn't know it by the hay belly she has."

He gazed in through the stall door at the horse. "Bring her out here so I can get a better look at her." A dozen possibilities clicked through his brain as his eyes covered every inch of the mare, but one by one he ruled them out. The horse's belly was the only thing that had any excess weight on it. She wasn't as thin as the black stallion, but she wasn't far behind.

Suddenly Jarrod straightened. "I wonder," he mumbled. He spun around and went back to his truck. He returned moments later wearing a shoulder-length surgical glove.

"What do you think it is? What are you doing?" Cassie burst out.

"I'll let you know in a minute." He lifted the mare's tail and slowly edged his hand inside her. "Just make sure you keep her still."

All at once, she figured out what Jarrod was checking for. "You think she's pregnant, don't you?" she asked in amazement.

He withdrew his arm and grinned. "Not just think. I know she is."

"It never occurred to me that could be why she had the big belly. Why wouldn't the woman we confiscated her from tell us she was bred?"

"Who knows? Maybe she wasn't sure herself. Or maybe she didn't want you to know there were two horses involved in being neglected."

Cassie shook her head, still in shock. "I'm surprised Les never—" She stopped herself as soon as she realized she'd spoken her thoughts aloud. The last thing she needed was for Jarrod to get a big head over this.

"I'm sure he would have very soon," Jarrod replied easily as he peeled off the glove. "She's far enough along now that it's really quite an obvious deduction if you look at it from a totally objective point of view. Les had seen her ever since you got her. At that time, being pregnant would have been the last thing to consider as the culprit. I would've thought her condition was from some other ailment then, too."

"I guess I better start giving her extra grain and hay." That was certainly an inane thing to say, she thought in disgust, but it was the first thing that had come to her frazzled mind. Jarrod Fitzgerald, humble? It didn't quite fit the image of him she'd carried with her these last few years.

"Along with a good supplement," Jarrod commented. "Now, any others?"

"Ah, no."

"What about that stallion?"

She met his defiant gaze, and for one split second considered giving in solely to keep things going pleasantly between them. But she did have to think of the horse first.

"Not today," she said.

"Why the hell not?"

"He's not ready for you yet. He's not even ready for me yet. If he won't take kindly to me touching his injuries, how do you think he'll take to you?"

Jarrod snorted. "You're not worried about him hurting me, you're worried about me hurting him. Say it. You don't trust me."

"I wouldn't say it's a matter of trust, exactly. I just don't think you have a very good attitude about him, and you know as well as I do how sensitive horses are about people's feelings. I can't count on how he would react around you."

Jarrod stepped forward until he was right in front of her. "I think there's more to it than that."

His face was so close to hers that she could feel his hot breath on her forehead. She resisted the temptation to back up. "Like what?"

"You're dangling that stallion at me like he's some sort of prize. You don't want to make everything here too easy for me, do you? The idea of being totally agreeable with me is more than you can take, isn't it?"

This time, Cassie didn't try to fight the temptation. She took a step backward. She didn't like the heat building inside her from being so near him. "That's not it—"

"You're ready to give that killer stallion more of a chance than you are me. At least I'm no danger to you physically."

She could have easily argued that point, but she didn't dare. She was more afraid of the pleasurable sensations he could arouse in her body than she was of the pain the stallion could cause her.

"You'll get to treat him eventually, just not today."

"Right."

"Look, if it's any consolation, I'm not sure I'd be able to have Les work on him yet either," she reasoned. "He has something against men, or maybe it's just vets. Right now it's more critical I win his trust than it is to stab him with a bunch of needles and alienate him further. Every other horse on this farm is vaccinated, so they can't catch anything. I'll just have to take my chances with his health until he settles in better. When that happens, I'll take a chance on you."

He was still skeptical, but he let the subject drop. "Can I take a look at him through the stall door?"

She sighed. "All right. But try not to do anything to get him worked up. It's taken me half a morning of babbling just to get him to where he doesn't freak out when I'm around."

Jarrod let Cassie lead the way, and he fell into step behind her. When they reached the stall, he saw the horse immediately flatten his ears and move into the corner. He listened for a moment while she spoke low, soothing words to the stallion, until another horse down the line whinnied quietly. The stallion's head went up and his ears pricked forward.

Jarrod froze, his full attention suddenly on the stallion. Cassie's voice became no more than a distant hum as he struggled to figure out what it was about the black rogue that all at once looked so familiar. Seconds later, the moment was lost when the stallion resumed his earlier hostile posture.

"What did you say his name was?" he asked with a frown.

Cassie felt her cheeks turn scarlet. "I call him Midnight. I don't know what his other name was."

"Midnight?" he repeated.

"What's wrong with that?"

"Nothing," he assured her as he tried to control his grin. Then his gaze returned to the horse, and his face sobered again thoughtfully. "I don't suppose you know if he has a tattoo under his lip?"

"I haven't exactly been buddy-buddy enough with him to look in his mouth yet."

"No, I guess you haven't. What's the name of the man who had him before?"

"Pete Erickson. Why?"

"Just curious." He shook his head. "I've never heard of him."

"You're not missing much, believe me."

"I believe you, but I'd still be interested in knowing if this horse has a tattoo to prove he's a registered Thorough-bred."

She started to ask him what difference it made when the look on his face stopped her. She knew it was the same look that had been on her face the day before. "You think he looks familiar, too, don't you?"

He glanced at her quickly, ready to pass it off until he saw her troubled expression. He hesitated briefly before he nodded. "Yes," he said simply. "I do."

"Now if we could only figure out who it is he reminds us of."

"Maybe if we pooled our thoughts, we could come up with something." Although dubious about the importance of such a discovery, it did provide him an opportunity he couldn't let get away. "I'm running a little behind today, so

I really do need to get going. How about dinner tomorrow night?''

"Dinner?"

"To discuss the horse."

Cassie was relieved to have a valid excuse. She didn't have to ponder the situation that way. "I have to work Friday night."

"Oh. Saturday night then?"

"I work on Saturday night, too."

"At the Country Club?"

"Yes." Her voice became guarded. "So?"

He couldn't keep from asking. It had never felt right to see her working at the Club. She was too classy to be waitressing for the wealthy. "Why do you work there?"

"That should be obvious," she retorted. "For the money."

"But—"

"I make good money there." She eyed him speculatively. "You see, most of the people who eat there are in the horse business. They knew my father or knew of him, and they all think they know what happened to Ebony Fire. They see Mike Malone's poor daughter working for a living in a restaurant, and they feel sorry for me. Not sorry enough to give me a job in any of their stables, mind you, but sorry enough to leave me very generous tips. I make more than any other waitress there."

"And it doesn't bother you? Their pity, I mean."

Her answering smile was genuine, and it told him she meant what she said. "It did at first. Until I realized the joke was on them. If they wanted to give me juicy tips to ease their consciences, why should I care? If I let their attitudes get me down, then it would only prove them right, that I was beneath them and deserved their pity. But that's not true. And so I make some extra money for my horses because of their insecurities."

Jarrod could only shake his head in appreciation. "You're something else."

"So I've been told. But not always favorably."

"Well, this time it is. How about dinner Sunday night?"

The time had come to ponder. "I don't know..." she hedged.

"Consider it strictly business. Maybe if you get to know me better, you'll find out I'm not as bad as you think I am. Then you'd feel better about having me as your vet."

"Just one little business dinner?"

He shrugged and gave her his most appealing smile. "It's as good a place as any to start, don't you think?"

Her eyes traveled from his dimpled cheeks to his sparkling eyes to his full mouth, and she felt herself weakening. She was dying to know why Midnight struck a familiar chord in both of them. And if he really was going to be her new vet, it would help their working relationship tremendously if she could relieve the animosity she felt toward him. The past could never be forgotten, but perhaps the time had come after all to start to forgive.

"Okay," she said with a dauntless grin of her own. "I'll go. On one condition."

Jarrod groaned. "What?"

"That I get to pick where we eat."

"Okay," he said. "Where do you want to go?"

"The Country Club."

One eyebrow raised in speculation. "You want to work there Friday and Saturday night, and then eat there on Sunday?"

"Sure. Is there a problem with that?"

"Not on my part." His smile deepened. "Lady, you've got yourself a date."

Three

Cassie spent the rest of the afternoon with the stallion. She brought a radio out from the house, set it in front of his stall, and tuned in an easy listening station. Perched next to it on a tall stool, she alternately talked to the horse or simply stared at him when he wasn't watching her. It took him nearly an hour before he relaxed enough to stand with one hind foot cocked and eyes half closed. It was then, when he looked the most peaceful, that he also looked the most pathetic. What she wouldn't give to be able to brush out his coat, tend to his cuts, and smooth away his distrust of the world in general and her in particular.

She wasn't aware she'd dozed off until the sound of the stallion blowing air through his nose woke her up with a start. Cassie watched in amusement as he tucked his head to his chest and arched his neck and back just like a newly awakened cat. Only the horse let out a tiny groan as he did so, reminding her unnecessarily that he didn't have the inherent flexibility of his feline counterpart.

"Surprised to find me still here, big guy?" she murmured. His ears flicked forward and then back again, but he didn't pin them. She took a deep breath. "Feel like having some company in there? Now is as good a time as any, seeing as how we both just woke up from a little nap."

The stallion eyed her warily as she slipped into his stall. He was already in the corner, so he couldn't retreat any farther. Cassie leaned casually against the stall door and talked softly to him. He merely allowed her presence; he didn't get aggressive but he didn't let down his guard either.

For the moment, Cassie was satisfied with that small amount of progress. She remained in the roomy box stall with him for fifteen long minutes before she turned and left. Tomorrow would be soon enough to get closer to him.

As she started her evening chores, she couldn't help but think about what stage she'd be at with the stallion if Jarrod hadn't made his untimely arrival yesterday. She really believed the horse would've taken the apple core from her. Instead, he'd blown up and associated her with Jarrod. Now she'd have to work extra hard to win the stallion's trust.

Trust. It seemed apparent that Jarrod was intent on earning hers. Did he think one dinner was going to do it? A thousand dinners probably wouldn't accomplish that goal. She'd learned her lesson a long time ago about trusting people associated with the racehorse business. Look where it had gotten her father.

So why had she agreed to go out to eat with Jarrod? She'd gotten along wonderfully with Les, and she'd never had dinner with him. Of course, Les hadn't callously accused her father of killing a horse, either. Les hadn't helped get her father fired. And Les had been a kind, compassionate vet, someone she could count on to give sensitive care to her horses.

For the hundredth time in the last twenty-four hours, she wondered if she'd done the right thing. But when her mind conjured up a flashing pair of dimples and stormy gray eyes, a sinewy muscled body and strong yet gentle hands, she realized she'd had no choice. It might not be the most rational decision she'd ever made in her life, but for better or worse, Jarrod Fitzgerald was now her vet.

"Well, we're here." Jarrod turned off the engine in his truck and glanced around the crowded Country Club's parking lot. "You're sure you want to eat at this place?"

Cassie turned in the seat of the pickup and sent him a challenging smile. "Sure, I'm sure. The food's excellent and the atmosphere is nice. What's the matter, don't you want to be seen here with me?"

"The way you look, I wouldn't mind being seen with you anywhere," he said gruffly, his eyes roaming over her.

He'd thought her jeans and T-shirt had enhanced her figure, but they were nothing compared to the lacy pink silk blouse she wore tonight tucked into a slim black skirt. Black high heels brought her height to within inches of his own, he'd noticed when he walked her to his truck earlier. She'd applied a trace of makeup to her sapphire eyes, which gave them even more dramatic depth. A softly scented, decidedly feminine fragrance clung to her, and it had teased his nose all the way to the Country Club. He hoped he would be able to keep his mind on his food tonight instead of on devouring her.

Cassie stirred uneasily under his bold scrutiny. The answer he'd given wasn't quite the one she wanted to hear, and it brought an unwelcome flush to her cheeks. "You shouldn't mind being seen with me because of who I am, not because of what I look like," she chastised him sharply.

"Oh." He grinned. "Did I forget to mention that part of it?"

She threw him an impudent look before reaching for the door handle. "Let's go in. I'm starving."

"Me too," he muttered, but at the moment his stomach was not the part of his anatomy making its hunger known.

The maître'd beamed at them both when they walked in the door. "Cassie!" he exclaimed in pleasure, then winked at her. "What in the world are you doing here with this guy?"

"Just a business dinner, Bernie," she said. "Dr. Fitzgerald is my new vet."

"You don't say," the maître'd replied thoughtfully. "Jarrod, I've never seen you bring any of your other clients here for a—what do you call it?—business dinner."

Jarrod put his arm over the robust man's shoulders. "Well, Bernie," he explained with a rakish smile, "that's because I've never had to tell any of my other clients it's a business dinner to get them to go out with me."

"Mr. Hot Shot here is only kidding, Bernie," Cassie remarked indifferently. "Of course it's only business. How about showing us to our table?"

Cassie tried to ignore Jarrod's hand on her elbow as they followed Bernie through the dining area. He sat them at a picturesque table by the floor-to-ceiling windows that overlooked some of Kentucky's greenest rolling hills. It was a lovely view, but she didn't even take notice of it because she was too preoccupied with Jarrod's offhanded comment. Did he really have more than business on his mind? The way he'd been looking at her tonight, she could easily believe it. She fervently hoped she wasn't staring at him the same way.

It was hard not to, she had to admit. He looked magnificently male in his navy slacks, gray sport coat, pale blue shirt, and striped tie. His neatly styled brown hair was still damp from a shower, which for some reason added to the enticing air of him. More often than not she preferred the casual look of a man in jeans, but Jarrod nearly took her breath away dressed the way he was tonight. She felt an almost overpowering desire to touch him. Would she be able to feel his steely muscles beneath the heavy sleeve of his sport coat? she wondered. What would his sculpted thighs feel like under the smooth fabric of his cotton slacks?

Cassie swallowed guiltily and opened her menu. She gazed unseeingly at the choices she knew by heart anyway and mentally shook herself. Those kind of thoughts were dangerous and stupid. And, infuriating as it was, impossible to banish. Damn it, it was all his fault! If he didn't make her feel so sensual with just one heated glance, then she wouldn't think of him with such ridiculous romantic delusions.

"What do you recommend?"

His husky voice sparked her senses and further ignited the irritation she felt toward him. "You've been here before," she snapped. "You should know what's good."

"Excuse me." Jarrod gazed at her curiously over the top of his menu. Her eyes rose briefly to meet his, then just as quickly flitted away.

She should apologize. It would be the decent thing to do. But every time Cassie opened her mouth, the words refused to come out. Then she was thankfully saved from the awkward moment by the appearance of Denise, their waitress.

"Cassie!" the young woman said with a chuckle. "You're the last person I expected to see here on a Sunday. Weren't the last two nights here enough for you?"

"They were certainly enough as a waitress, but it's kind of interesting to be on the other end once in a while."

"Especially with an attractive date like this one," Denise said.

"Well, actually—" Cassie started to correct her, but Jarrod cut her off.

"Thank you," he said easily. "I find Cassie quite interesting, too." He gave her a look that dared her to bring up business again.

"Jarrod's my new vet," she countered smoothly, not quite discounting him, but not quite agreeing with him either. "I think I told you about Les retiring."

"Yeah, you did. That was a shame. I know how close you were to him. 'Course, it looks like you're off to a good start with his replacement."

Jarrod knew Cassie wouldn't let that remark slide. "I think we're ready to order," he interjected hastily. As soon as Denise left with their dinner choices, he turned the conversation around. "So how's that killer stallion of yours?"

"Midnight? He's not a killer."

"Okay. So how's that gentle stallion of yours?"

"He's not gentle yet either. But he's coming along quite well. I brushed him out this morning."

"Really? And he didn't mind?"

"At first he wasn't too thrilled. But I had him in crossties, and he settled down and stood quietly after a while." After a long while, actually, but she was enjoying the impressed look on his face too much to give out the exact details.

"That's great. When can I treat him?"

"Not yet. He's just getting used to me. I don't want to spoil that by having you upset him again."

"Have you given any thought to gelding him? It would be easier on both of you."

"Maybe. Well, probably. But it's too soon for me to make that kind of decision. When I get him rehabilitated, he'll be worth more as a stallion."

"He'll be easier to sell as a gelding. You don't have any papers on him anyway. He's no good to anyone as a stud."

Cassie toyed with the tiny drops of condensation that had formed on her crystal water glass instead of responding to his reasonable argument. How could she tell him it didn't feel right to geld Midnight? He'd had so much taken away from him already. Even though it would undoubtedly calm and settle him, she didn't think she could do him the final injustice of castrating him. She could never expect Jarrod to understand any of that, so she didn't even attempt to explain it.

"Did you remember anything more about him?" she asked at last.

"The stallion?"

"Yes. You thought he looked familiar. Did you ever figure out why?"

"No. And I've wracked my brain trying to place him. How about you?"

"I haven't had any luck either. It shouldn't be so hard, because there aren't that many black Thoroughbreds around."

"But we're not sure he's Thoroughbred," he pointed out.

"We've both seen enough Thoroughbreds in our lives to know one when we see one. Midnight's a Thoroughbred all right."

"I'll believe it when I see his tattoo. If you'd let me get close enough to him to give him a tranquilizer, we'd find out a lot sooner."

"He'd never hold still enough for you to get an IV needle in his neck," she contended. "I should be able to get a look under his lip by the end of the week. Then at least I can trace the registration number down and find out a little more about him."

"Just be careful," he warned. "Those teeth can remove quite a mouthful of skin."

"I appreciate your concern, but I know what I'm doing. I've worked with horses like him before." At his arched brow, she amended her statement. "Okay, so not quite like him, but close enough to know the best way to handle him. I'll be fine."

"Just remember you have other horses depending on you at your farm besides that stallion. If you let your guard down around him and he takes advantage of it, all your animals will be affected if you're too injured to take care of them."

Cassie smiled slowly. He knew right where to aim his appeal so it would be the most effective. She found it both flattering and frightening that he had that much insight about her. "I really do know what I'm doing. If you knew me better, you wouldn't worry so much."

He smiled meaningfully back at her. "I'd like very much to know you better." His eyes locked with hers for what seemed an eternity.

"Here's your salads," Denise announced cheerfully. "And your diet colas."

Cassie was grateful for the interruption. She was sure now that she'd unglued her eyes from Jarrod's, her pulse would stop its racing and drop down to a steady jog. She downed half of her soda, hoping to cool off her suddenly fevered body.

"I've always liked the soda here," she explained lamely, noticing Jarrod's gaze resting oddly on her half-empty glass.

"Would you like another one?"

"Not right now, thanks."

Jarrod took a large swallow of his own cola. "You're right, it is pretty good. I usually drink something else when I come here, but I'm on call tonight."

"You are?" Of course. That's why he'd picked her up in his fully equipped truck and wasn't drinking anything stiffer. A flicker of disappointment went through her, knowing he could be whisked away from her at any moment by his beeper.

"Yeah. But I'm not expecting any emergencies tonight." He laughed. "I shouldn't have said that, because whenever I think everything is going to be peaceful, that's just when all hell breaks loose."

"I suppose you get called out a lot after regular hours since you have so many clients. In fact, I imagine you're quite a busy man. So, why did you really agree to take over my account from Les?" she asked with quiet firmness. "What's in it for you?"

He casually lifted his glass up to eye level and stared at the rising bubbles inside it as if his answer could be found there. Shrugging, he took a languid swallow of soda before he responded. "Why does there have to be anything in it for me?"

"You didn't think much of the Malones when Ebony Fire died. Why should you want to help one out now?"

"The truth?"

She nodded and held her breath.

"I don't know."

She expelled the air out of her lungs in a frustrated sigh. "That's not telling the truth. That's being evasive."

"No, it isn't," he insisted seriously. "It's the truth. I can't tell you one overwhelming reason why I agreed. There were a lot of little reasons, but—"

"For instance?" she probed.

Jarrod knew she wouldn't appreciate hearing he'd become her vet partially out of remorse. He skirted the issue. "Oh, like I thought your work was worthwhile and it would be a good thing for me to do, especially since I've been a little short in the unselfish department lately. Besides that, I knew how important it was to Les."

"I didn't realize you knew him that well."

"I served one of my internships under Les for a whole summer. A lot of established vets don't like to take the time to really teach a student while also giving them the opportunity to learn. Les wasn't like that. I learned half of what I know from him."

"You couldn't have had a better teacher."

"Les was the best overall vet I've ever known."

About to delve further, Cassie was forced to wait as Denise showed up with their dinner.

"Did you happen to notice the snake that just slithered in?" Denise whispered venomously to Cassie as she set the plate down in front of her.

Cassie stiffened immediately. There was only one man she and Denise referred to that way. Her eyes drifted over toward the maître'd stand where they met with the icy glare of Nathan Hall's cool appraisal.

Jarrod watched her eyes freeze over and turned to see who she was looking at. Nate and his wife were at the other end of Cassie's stare. Nate's gaze drifted from Cassie to him, and even from that distance Jarrod could detect the surprise on the other man's face as recognition set in. Without another word to Bernie, Nate headed toward their table. Jarrod could sense the tension build in Cassie with every step Nate took. He turned his head and offered her a reassuring smile. She never noticed it.

"Enjoy your dinner," Denise mumbled before hurrying away.

"Cassandra, I didn't think you worked on Sundays," Nate said without preamble as soon as he reached their table. "Are you on break?"

"She's with me, Nate," Jarrod put in fluidly, rankled by the man's deliberate put-down. "How are you doing?"

"Fine, just fine." He turned to study Jarrod. "I didn't realize you were acquainted with Mike Malone's daughter."

"Dr. Fitzgerald is my new vet," Cassie said before Jarrod could respond.

"Is that so?" Nate commented with feigned interest. "He's quite expensive. How are you getting him to discount his rates for you, Cassandra?"

Jarrod had to give her credit. She didn't gasp, didn't shrink away in embarrassment, didn't back down. Her eyes narrowed to dangerous slits, and he could feel her outrage charge the atmosphere around them. Yet she kept her cool. If he wasn't so fascinated watching her, he might have jumped up and punched his most lucrative client in the mouth.

"Really, Nate, such petty cattiness is unworthy of you," Cassie replied with mock sweetness. "Not everyone has to achieve personal gain in order to contribute to a worthy cause. But you wouldn't know about that, would you?"

"Yeah, Nate, give me the benefit of the doubt, will you?" With an effort, Jarrod forced his voice to remain pleasant. "I do have a few unselfish bones in my body."

"Of course you do." Nate shrugged, and for all practical appearances, he looked totally bored with their conversation. "Well, I'll see you tomorrow at the usual time, Jarrod. And Miss Malone, I'll look forward to seeing you again soon, too. Perhaps next Friday night, when your position here will be reversed?"

"You might see me, but I won't be waiting on *your* table."

Nate laughed and walked away to rejoin his wife. Only when he was seated with his back to her did Cassie start to relax. She sighed and smiled briefly at the striking man sitting across from her, who was watching her with a mixture of amusement and respect on his face.

"I'm sorry," she said.

"For what?"

"I shouldn't let him get to me so much, but I just can't be civil to that man."

He reached over and covered her small trembling hand with his much larger one. "I think you handled him just right, and exactly how he deserved. I should be the one apologizing to you."

Cassie tried not to study the natural picture his hand made on hers, but her eyes refused to look away. She resisted the impulse to rotate her fingers so they could entwine with his. There was no sense spoiling the image he had of her as tough.

"Why should you apologize to me?" she asked after a moment. "You backed me up."

"Not as much as I should have. I guess I was just too stunned to see Nate acting that way. It's a side of him I've never seen." He took his hand away from hers and leaned back in his chair. "What does he have against you anyway? Surely he can't have such hostile feelings toward you simply because of your father."

"No, that's only part of it." Her hand was tingling warmly and she rested it in her lap until it stopped. "We had some pretty heated arguments about what happened to Ebony Fire. Despite what you think, my father thought the world of that horse and he would never have been irresponsible with his care. Nate never appreciated my arguments in my father's defense."

"The rumor was Mike had been drinking that night."

"Rumors!" Cassie let out a short, scornful laugh. "Was that the one you chose to believe? No, my father had been on prescription drugs from a bout with pneumonia, and that's why he was a little foggy about it all the next morning. But he told me he distinctly remembered everything being completely fine when he turned in for the night, and I've never doubted him. I'm sure Nate started the drinking rumors, although I've never figured out why." She smiled grimly. "I accused Nate of some pretty horrible things at the time, and then even more when my father died. I don't regret one word. And I don't doubt the validity of a single thing I said to him, either."

"Like what?"

"Oh, no you don't. You're not going to get me going on all of that. He is one of your clients, remember?"

"You don't think I'd run and tell him everything you told me, do you?"

"It wouldn't matter if you did. He's heard it all before."

"Then why won't you tell me what you think he's guilty of?"

"Because it's past history. Granted, it's not forgotten, but I don't like to think about it anymore, let alone talk about it. Besides, what good would it do? I doubt you'd believe me over him anyway."

That elicited more hurt than anger, but it was only the anger he was willing to acknowledge. And show. "How can you say that? I know Nate's not a stellar member of our society. If we're going to have any kind of relationship at all, you're going to have to get over this damn habit of thinking the worst about me all the time. I—"

"Jarrod—"

"I'm not finished yet! I—"

"Jarrod!"

"What?"

"You're being beeped," she said quietly. At his blank expression, she elaborated. "Your beeper is going off. People are starting to stare."

"Oh." The incessant high-pitched beeping finally registered in his mind. He switched it off, cursing under his breath. "I'll be right back. I have to call my answering service."

Cassie grabbed his arm as he was going by. "What do you mean, 'if we're going to have any kind of a relationship'? Who said anything about us having a relationship?"

He grinned, the picture of innocence. "I was talking about a business relationship. What kind of relationship did you have in mind?"

She met his gaze, which at that moment was no small feat. "Why, business, of course. I just wanted to make sure that's what you had in mind."

"I see." The smug look on his face didn't diminish as he left to use the phone.

Cassie knew by the heat in her cheeks that they must be a vivid shade of red. She let out a deep breath and looked down at her steak dinner. Her untouched steak dinner. Jarrod's food was similarly intact. Her stomach was in such turmoil from memories of her father and dealing with Jarrod that the idea of taking even one bite now was unthinkable. She hoped Jarrod wasn't hungry either, because it appeared he was going to be called away without a chance to eat.

"Bad news, I'm afraid," Jarrod announced as he sat down on the edge of his chair. "A mare's gone into labor a couple weeks early, and the owner thinks it might be a breech birth because she's having quite a time of it. I have to leave right away. I'm really sorry."

"That's all right. I know it's part of your job. Will you have time to take me home?"

He frowned. "That's kind of a problem, because the stable I'm going to is completely in the opposite direction of your house. I can't really spare the time to go that much out of the way."

"I could ride along with you," she suggested hesitantly. "I could stay in your truck so I wouldn't be in the way."

"Cassie, this could go on most of the night, and there's no saying that I won't get another call later. You'd be bored silly."

"No, I wouldn't," she insisted. "I haven't seen a newborn foal in a long time. I wouldn't mind the wait."

"All right, if you're sure." Jarrod rose and pulled out his wallet. He dropped the appropriate number of bills on the table before reaching for her arm. "Let's go."

With her eyes trained straight ahead to avoid Nate's gaze, Cassie stayed close to Jarrod until they'd stepped out into the cool April evening air. Uncomfortable with the contact, she edged away then and welcomed the touch of the invigorating breeze on her flushed skin.

"I'm sorry about dinner," Jarrod said after they were on their way. "We can stop somewhere for a quick bite when this is all over."

"At least we had our salads."

"Rabbit food has never been enough to tide me over for very long. I guess it was better than nothing, though."

"Yes." Cassie stared unseeingly out the window, grateful for the darkness that kept her in shadows. Why did she feel so strained and jittery all of a sudden? Was it because her little business dinner seemed to have turned into something a whole lot more intimate?

"I hate to have you sit in the truck the whole time, but this particular mare is a bit leery of strangers," Jarrod went on. "I don't want her to be unnecessarily anxious over having any extra people around. She's not going to be very happy to have me there as it is."

"I know. I spent a lot of time with Thoroughbred brood mares over the years."

"And I'll bet they never minded having you around when they were delivering, did they?" He glanced over at her pointedly. "I don't remember seeing you much when I was called out to Nate's during a birth, though."

"I was close by." She fidgeted uneasily with the purse on her lap, hoping he would let the subject drop. Her hope was short-lived.

"You were always just out of sight, though, weren't you? You avoided me like the plague. Why?"

"You said yourself the past is best forgotten," she reminded him tersely. "Let's forget about this conversation."

"Okay, we will." He slowed the truck down and turned up the driveway that led to a multimillion-dollar racing stable. "For now."

Cassie kept silent as he parked next to one of the huge red barns. He got out and went to the back of the truck. After rummaging around for a few minutes, he walked to her side of the cab, his blue coveralls now in place over his dress clothes. He motioned with his hand for her to roll down her window.

She lowered the pane several inches. "What?"

"I'll be back as soon as I can. Try not to think up too creative an answer to my question while I'm gone."

"Take your time," she called out as he strode away. With a sigh, Cassie rolled the window down some more and hooked her arm over the outside of it. She rested her chin on her hand as a faint breeze caught her hair and blew it back out of her face.

Forget the past where it concerns Jarrod, she ordered herself. Yet how could she when he insisted on bringing it up all the time? Not that she really needed his reminders to get her memories into sharp focus again, anyway. She could no more forget the attraction she'd felt for Jarrod years ago than she could ignore it now.

She had avoided him at all costs back then, yet she couldn't get over the fact that he'd been aware of it. Once Jarrod had become Nate's vet, it hadn't taken her long to discover it was best to slip away whenever he drove up. Those steamy, intense gray eyes of his had seemed to hone in on her every time he came. It evoked a restlessness in her that she'd never been able to comprehend. Class differences had seemed monumental to her at the time, and her only recourse had been learning to melt into the woodwork.

In a strange way, it had been almost a relief to leave Nate's, even though it had happened in such a terrible way. Although she had to admit she'd missed seeing Jarrod at first, she'd somehow felt safer being completely away from him. She could remain in her own secure little world, emotions judiciously guarded and kept in control. And then, of course, bitterness over her father had emerged to dominate her other feelings.

Bitterness had survived uncontested for years. Not anymore.

Her thoughts drifted to the man in the barn, fighting to deliver a healthy foal. Was he the same person who'd accused her father so viciously of negligence when Ebony Fire died? It hardly seemed possible. But then, she thought wryly, it was no more implausible than finding herself practically on a date with that same man. She must be out of her mind.

"Cassie? Cassie, wake up."

She awoke with a start, disoriented for a moment after unknowingly falling asleep. Stifling a yawn, she shivered from the chilly air coming in through her still-open window. After a quick search of Jarrod's relaxed smile, she decided all must have gone well with the delivery.

"How's the foal?" she asked.

"Ready to get to her feet." He pulled open the door and held out his hand. "Want to watch?"

She nodded, instantly fully awake and alert. "I'd love to."

Jarrod helped her step out of the truck and then released her hand. "Wait here a second." He left her to dig in the back of his truck and returned with his sport coat. "Put this on. You look like you're half frozen."

"Thanks." As he guided her arms into the sleeves, Cassie noticed his torrid gaze pinned to the front of her. She glanced down to see her nipples, taut and peaked, clearly evident beneath the pink lace of her blouse as the fabric clung to her breasts. With a jerk, she hurriedly finished putting on his jacket and wrapped the thick material tightly around her upper body. Despite her crossed arms and the sudden warmth, she trembled.

"I'm, uh, glad you got some sleep while you were waiting." Jarrod stumbled over the words, unable to tear his eyes away from her. The outdoor spotlight illuminated her lovely glowing face and danced among the black waves of her hair. He was still reeling from the glimpse he'd had of her budded nipples. It had hit him with all the force of a savage blow to his stomach.

"It's a filly?"

It was an effort to get his thoughts back on track. "What?"

"The foal. You called it a her."

"Oh." He exhaled and drew up a smile. "Yes. She's a real beauty. Come on, I'll show you."

Cassie followed him into the dimly lit barn. He stopped in front of a large box stall near the end of the aisle. She peered inside, her breath catching at once. Nestled in a pile of clean straw lay a light brown, spindly legged filly. Her coat, no more than soft downy fuzz, was being licked dry by her dark chestnut mother.

"She's gorgeous!" Cassie exclaimed in a hushed whisper. Tiny brown ears flicked in her direction simultaneously with the mare's. The new mother immediately returned her attention to nuzzling her foal.

"Just like I told you."

Cassie stopped staring at the delicate filly long enough to notice they were alone in the barn. "Where's the owner?"

"He went back up to the house. He stayed out here long enough to see what sex the foal was. Once he knew it wasn't a colt, he left."

"So he doesn't care about this beautiful baby because it's a female," Cassie said flatly. She'd seen that attitude among racehorse owners before, and it never failed to enrage her.

Jarrod shrugged. "Colts stand to make a lot more money at the track than fillies, and again later standing at stud. It's a matter of economics, you know that."

"I don't care. Someone should still be here to appreciate that miniature miracle in there whether it's male or female."

"We're here, Cassie." He wrapped his arm around her shoulder and pulled her gently to his side. "That baby couldn't have a more appreciative audience."

Miniscule jolts of electricity charged up and down her at the full-length contact with Jarrod's brawny body. His breath was warm against her ear, and she wanted nothing more than to give in to the yearning to lay her head against his massive chest. To keep from doing just that, she concentrated fiercely on the new filly. The foal did her share to help by choosing that moment to try to get to her feet for the first time.

Cassie watched with amusement and awe as the filly lurched up on her front legs, only to fall down before her back legs ever got a chance to assist. Her next few attempts were similarly unsuccessful, but finally, on her sixth try, the foal managed a swaying stance. A cautious step toward her mother left her tumbling to the straw again. She got up once more, and this time she made it to the mare's belly. In seconds, the filly located the full milk bag that was waiting to give her her first meal.

As she witnessed the filly suckling, Cassie felt her throat constrict with emotion. "I've seen it a hundred times in my life," she murmured reverently. "But every time is just as special as the first." She turned to look up into the smoldering depths of Jarrod's eyes. "Thank you for sharing this with me."

His mouth was physically being drawn to hers, Jarrod thought fleetingly as his head lowered until her lips met his.

He could no more have prevented it from happening than he could have walked to the moon. For as long as he could, he kept the contact fragile and tender, the way the moment seemed to dictate. When he felt her mouth respond with growing pressure, the kiss soon catalyzed into something much more ravishing. His lips moved over hers, thoroughly and hungrily, demanding her total captivation. She gave it willingly.

Cassie's hands roamed up around his neck, where they clasped together amidst the hair at his nape. She had no choice but to hang on to him as his mouth drained every ounce of strength out of her body. Never had she felt so weak and yet so powerful at the same time. All her senses heightened into glorious awareness—from the sweet smell of straw, to the tangy masculine taste of his mouth, to the sound of her own quiet moan.

Her, moaning? Hearing the evidence of her desire forced a rush of reality into her system, and she broke her mouth away from his. Still, she was left clinging to him as she struggled to regain badly needed oxygen.

Jarrod tipped his forehead down until it rested against hers. "I've waited years to kiss you like that," he confessed huskily. "And you know what?"

"What?"

"It was worth it."

She closed her eyes. "Jarrod, I—"

"Why did you avoid me all that time at Nate's?" he interrupted. "This could've happened a long time ago."

"I wasn't ready for this a long time ago." Then she shook her head and smiled dryly as she moved away from him. "What am I saying? I'm not ready for it now. I think you should take me home."

"I'll be happy to, as soon as you answer my question."

"It's not worth going into," she said. "It all happened so long ago, what difference could it make?"

"It makes a difference to me." He propped himself up lazily against the stall. "I've got all night to hear your explanation."

She hated being pushed into doing anything, but she recognized the stubborn will in Jarrod that just might match her own. "You and I were from two completely different worlds," she began.

"That's ridiculous. You can't tell me that's all there was to it."

"Can't I? How would you know what it was like to be a groom's daughter, to be a lowly groom yourself? How could you understand what it was like to get dated by the son of a very rich racehorse owner? To get wined and dined, then get dropped when he decided to find someone else to get serious with who was closer to his class?"

Jarrod's brow furrowed. "I never heard about you dating someone like that."

"Of course you didn't. He wouldn't take me any place where we'd run into anyone in his circle, and that included the Country Club."

"He wouldn't take you there?" *No wonder she'd told him she wanted to eat at the Club. She'd been testing him.* "Who was this jerk, anyway?"

"He's not worthy of my repeating his name." Her gaze turned on Jarrod assessingly. "It wasn't long after he dumped me that you took over as Nate's vet. The parallels between you and him were unmistakable. I had no desire to get slapped in the face twice, so I stayed as far from you as I could."

"You really thought you weren't good enough for me?" he asked in amazement.

"No, *I* never thought that. But I was afraid *you* might think it."

"You wouldn't even give me the benefit of the doubt back then?"

"Not at that time I wouldn't, but don't worry. I don't even think about such things now."

"Good, I—"

"That's because I've come to the conclusion that you're the one who's not good enough for me, so there's no problem."

He reached out and pulled her to him in an instant. "Lucky for you, I know you have a terrific sense of humor," he replied, his gaze holding hers captive. "Otherwise, I might have to give you a demonstration to show you just how compatible we really are."

Somehow, her story and her teasing had backfired on her. Jarrod appeared ready to ravage her mouth again, and Cassie wasn't at all sure she could survive that another time tonight. What had happened to the suave, assertive woman she liked to think she'd grown into? She hadn't known just how accurate she'd been when she told Jarrod she still wasn't ready for anything to develop between them. She might not be leery of class differences anymore, but she was terrified of losing herself in such intense passion.

"You said you'd take me home," Cassie objected, attempting to wiggle free of his arms.

"Whatever you say." Jarrod released every part of her but one hand. He gripped it firmly and looked in on the foal one last time. "The filly shouldn't need me for anything else tonight. She's doing great."

Cassie only wished she herself were doing as well. By the time they reached the truck, her pulse rate was still hammering away in double time. Between the dramatic birth of a new foal and the fervor in Jarrod's kiss, her emotions were a mess. Relief filled her on the way home when Jarrod apparently decided to keep quiet throughout the drive and let her think.

As they pulled into her driveway, Cassie took in a deep breath. What would she be in store for now that the evening was over and they'd be forced to talk to each other? She mentally calculated how fast she could run in her high heels. Not fast enough, she decided woefully.

"I forgot to ask you if you wanted to stop somewhere to eat on the way back," Jarrod said, shifting into park.

"That's okay," she returned in a rush. "I'd probably get sick eating at one in the morning, anyway."

Jarrod flashed her a grin. "Not me. I can eat any time, day or night. Which is a good thing, I guess, considering my schedule."

"Yes, well, I better let you go. I'm sure you need to get some sleep before your day starts again in a few hours." Her fingers were already on the door handle when she felt his hand on her elbow. She opened the door before turning to glance at him.

"I'm glad you were with me tonight," he told her softly. "Sometimes I take a delivery a little nonchalantly because I've seen so many. I didn't do that with you there." He withdrew his hand and offered her a slow, simmering smile. "Sleep well. I'll stop by tomorrow to see if you need anything."

"Good night." The words flew from her mouth as she jumped out of the truck. She'd reached the front door before realizing Jarrod hadn't budged. Was he waiting to see if she got inside all right, or was he waiting to see if she'd change her mind and invite him in? Either way, he got his answer as she hastily unlocked the door and stepped into the house without looking back.

Cassie tossed her purse and keys on the kitchen table and headed for the refrigerator. She desperately needed a can of soda to ease her parched throat. Popping the top, she took a long drink and then restlessly paced around the room.

How had she gotten herself into this? Why had she ever been foolish enough to agree to let Jarrod be her vet? She should've realized what she was setting herself up for. Too much of her life had revolved around her father, Nate, and Ebony Fire for her to continue on in a simplistic way, now that Jarrod was back reminding her of everything.

If only she could have convinced her father years ago to look for work somewhere else besides Nate's stable. She'd never liked Nathan Hall, but her father had proven to be very stubborn on the subject. He'd once told her Nate had some of the best horses in all of Kentucky, and although he could find something to love about any horse, he especially enjoyed working with the top of the line. And top of the line had certainly described Ebony Fire.

A man like Nate didn't deserve a champion Thoroughbred like Ebony Fire, she thought, fuming over what had been a sore spot with her for years. She could still see that exquisite horse in her mind even now. The first moment she'd laid eyes on him had been enough to show her why her father had thought he was so special.

That horse had such a proud elegance about him, she recalled fondly. She had no better word to describe him than arrogant, despite the fact that such a term was usually reserved for people. Ebony Fire had been first class all the way, and he'd known it. The way his sleek black hide glistened over rippling muscles, the way he tossed his head when he was impatient or simply feeling good, the majestic way he moved even while just walking, were all forever stamped in her memory.

He was the most breathtaking horse she'd ever seen, and it was nothing less than a tragedy that he had died so young, before he'd ever passed on some of his magnificent genes. What she wouldn't give to have owned one of his foals, or even Ebony Fire himself. She could picture him on her farm now, galloping gallantly around one of her paddocks...

All at once, realization hit her, and the resulting shock was so overwhelming that her fingers lost the grip on the can she was holding. It slipped to the floor, fizzed-up cola shooting everywhere. Completely oblivious to the wet spray on her legs, she stood there trying to refute what she knew was undeniably a fact, no matter how impossible it seemed.

The rogue stallion that was in her barn right now, the horse that had barely been alive when she'd gotten him days ago, the horse that had been driving her crazy because he reminded her so much of another horse . . . was none other than Ebony Fire himself.

Four

————

Cassie threw open the front door and sprinted to the barn as best she could in her pumps. She hadn't taken the time to change shoes, not wanting to waste a second longer than was necessary to take a closer look at Midnight.

No, she corrected herself, not Midnight. Ebony Fire.

She heaved the sliding barn door open and switched on every light she had. The walkway and all the stalls were instantly bathed in blinding brightness, and she had to squint until her eyes adjusted to the contrast of the dark night she'd just left behind. Several horses poked curious noses over the stall doors, their eyes likewise blinking rapidly against the sudden intrusion of light.

Cassie's heels created a staccato echoing on the concrete as she marched down to the last stall. She hadn't expected a greeting from the stallion, and she didn't get one. He was resting in the corner of his stall, but one ear did flick casually forward to acknowledge her presence at the door.

Goosebumps rose on every inch of her flesh as she stared at the horse.

"It just can't be," she whispered over her pounding heartbeat.

But it was. She knew in her soul she was right, even though it was so completely incredible. The stallion's massive size, tiny ears, delicate facial structure, high tail carriage, and thick joints were all identical to her memory of Ebony Fire. He even had a white mark on his forehead, as had Ebony Fire. Certainly the two horses' attitudes matched. Her gaze dropped to the stallion's back legs and centered on his right rear foot. White hair covered his pastern and most of his fetlock. Cassie frowned. She didn't think Ebony Fire had had any white socks. She pushed the thought aside for the moment.

"Oh, Bonfire," she murmured, unconsciously using her father's pet name for the horse. The stallion's ears darted forward alertly. Just a coincidence, she told herself firmly. He wouldn't have heard the name in years, and she wasn't about to let herself use his reaction to that word as further proof she was right.

It didn't matter anyway. Horses seldom responded to their names like a dog or cat, so whether or not Ebony Fire remembered his other name wasn't important. When she got him healthy and feeling good again and she could watch him run, then she would have all the proof she needed. She would never, ever forget how that horse moved.

A smile lit up her face as she walked slowly out of the barn. There was one other thing she could do to build her case. If that stallion was Ebony Fire, the tattoo under his lip would verify it. All she had to do was get friendly enough with him so he'd let her look.

Cassie turned off the lights in the barn and trailed thoughtfully back up to the house. In minutes she'd traded her dress clothes for a fleece bathrobe. She wandered into the den and hesitated in front of the bifold closet doors. Her hands were shaking as she pulled open the doors and stood on tiptoe to reach one of the photo albums on the top shelf. She carried it with her to the bedroom and climbed in beneath the security of the heavy quilt on her bed. Immediately, one of her cats leapt up beside her and settled in a comforting, purring ball at her feet.

Cassie sighed as she gently brushed some of the dust off the album's cover. It was an unnecessary reminder of how long it had been since she'd looked at the pictures inside. Some memories were still painful for her, and photos of her smiling, happy father with his horses definitely fell into that category. She bit down on her bottom lip and opened the album.

By the time she'd gone through several pages, her eyes became moist, blurring the photos in front of her. The tears pooled quickly and overflowed onto the plastic pages that protected the images of the man who'd been both mother and father to her almost as long as she could remember. Her mother, who was no more than a dim but pleasant memory now, had died in a boating accident when Cassie was six. She'd been left with a father whose days off were few and far between, a father whose career took him frequently to racetracks where his primary attention was by necessity centered on horses instead of a little girl.

Not that she'd ever felt slighted in life. Mike Malone had loved her enough for two parents. He'd nurtured her through the times early on when she often turned sullen over the loss of her mother, all the way through to her sometimes stormy and uncertain times as a teenager. He'd taught her how to ride, how to laugh, and how to live. Lord, how she missed him.

Cassie wiped her eyes so she could study a picture of her father standing next to Ebony Fire. The photo, taken with a cheap instamatic camera, wasn't in sharp focus, but she could see the horse had four black feet. Still, everything else about him was the same as the horse in her barn, except for the three hundred pounds of body weight that her stallion was lacking. Her gaze drifted back to the proud man hold-

ing the lead rope. It was one of the last pictures she'd taken
of him.

She closed the book and squeezed her eyes tightly shut.
She hated to cry. It wasn't that she considered it a sign of
weakness, but it was so unproductive. Crying was supposed to make a person feel better, but it always had the
opposite effect on her. She set the photo album on the
nightstand next to her bed and turned off the lamp. She re-
settled herself under the covers, disturbing the sleeping
black cat at her feet. It crawled up to snuggle against her
side.

She was stroking it absently when her hand suddenly froze
in mid-air. If Ebony Fire was alive, then her father obviously was not responsible for his death! What better proof
of her father's innocence could there be? She had all the
evidence she needed right in her very own barn to clear his
name and resurrect his reputation. Somehow, Nathan Hall
had pulled off a very lucrative scam. He'd publicly blamed
her father for the champion racehorse's death and collected the insurance money without the horse ever dying.
And now she'd ended up with the horse.

How ironic, she thought with sweet pleasure.

How unbelievable, she corrected herself with gloomy
reality.

Who wouldn't think she was out of her mind for suggest-
ing such a thing? Even Jarrod wasn't likely to believe her,
and he thought her stallion looked familiar, too. But Jarrod had been Ebony Fire's vet, and surely he'd see the resemblance eventually. Perhaps she'd drop a few hints
tomorrow and see if she could trigger his memory without
actually coming right out and telling him her theory.

Tomorrow. If she didn't get some sleep, she'd be in no
shape to do anything tomorrow. But merely telling herself
to relax was futile. She had too much to keep her whirling
mind occupied. Finally, only hours before dawn, exhaustion overtook her. She dozed off into a dream-filled sleep
where she galloped carefree on a jet black stallion as her fa-

ther and Jarrod Fitzgerald watched with shared smiles and pride.

The excited family of four was just pulling out of her driveway with their newly adopted Thoroughbred mare in tow when Jarrod drove in. Cassie sighed, pushing away the melancholy she always felt after letting one of her rehabilitated horses go, and slipped the check she'd received into the back pocket of her jeans.

Jarrod stepped out of the truck and cocked his head in the direction of the disappearing trailer. "Who was that?"

"Good morning to you, too."

"Pardon my rudeness," he remarked with a mocking bow. "Good morning."

He looked haggard, she thought. Like he'd had about as much sleep as she had. "Those were the Richardsons. They just bought one of my mares."

She looked anxious, he thought. Restless. Like something was bothering her. He wondered if it was related to him or the sale of that horse. "Nice family?"

"Of course. I wouldn't have sold them a horse otherwise." Her gaze roamed unconsciously to the end of the driveway. It was silly to miss the mare already, but she did.

"Oh, by the way, our new little filly is doing fine today. I stopped by there this morning and checked on her."

"That's good," she said distractedly. Had it only been a mere matter of hours since she and Jarrod had been with the newborn foal? A mere matter of hours since he'd kissed her? Today it almost seemed like it had never happened. She glanced up at Jarrod, only to find him watching her intently. Her eyes darted away.

Jarrod swept past her into the barn. Her message to forget what happened the night before couldn't have been any clearer. Strangely disappointed, he chose to let it go. "Well, how's everybody in here doing today?"

Cassie stared after him a moment before following him inside. "Everybody's doing just fine," she answered for the horses. "In fact, I don't need you to do anything for me today."

Boy, did he have a comeback for that one. But he decided it was far wiser to keep his tongue. "How's Killer?"

Cassie's heart leapt into her throat. "Go see for yourself," she said with forced casualness.

"Really? You aren't going to yell at me to stay away from him today?"

"I didn't say you could go in his stall, I just said you could look at him."

Jarrod reached the stallion's stall and studied him for a while. "At least he's settling down some," he commented. The stallion was the calmest he'd seen him so far. "When do you plan on letting me treat him?"

"I don't have an exact date in mind."

"What about today?"

She shook her head. "I don't think he's far enough along yet."

"He's not far enough along? Or is it just that I haven't made enough points with you yet and you still don't trust me?"

"How many times do we have to go over this?" She leaned back against the stall and crossed her arms over her chest. "It has nothing to do with you personally."

"Really? Then prove it."

One corner of Cassie's mouth twisted up into a slight smile. "How?"

"Let me treat him right now."

"Why is this so important to you?"

Jarrod looked past her into the stall. "It's my job to help your horses. There isn't another horse on your farm that needs my help more than he does."

"There's more to it than that," she scoffed.

"Cassie, I'm a good vet, you know that. Your stallion wouldn't be the first horse I've ever worked on who hated vets." His voice softened, along with his eyes. "I know it won't go smoothly, but the amount his health will suffer is going to compound every day you put me off."

How much longer could she hold out? How much longer could she deny that what he said made perfect sense? With a sigh of resignation, she admitted to herself that it was time to give in. "All right," she grumbled. "I'll bring him out in the aisle while you get whatever you need out of your truck."

"Thank you," he said, eyeing the stallion as he turned away. "I think."

Steeling herself against the battle to come, Cassie snapped a lead rope onto the stallion's halter and brought him out of the stall. The horse sidestepped around her but didn't try to bite. When Jarrod approached them a moment later, hands laden with syringes and antiseptic, the stallion lurched backward in an effort to get away. Giving the lead rope several jerks, Cassie got him forward again.

"Take it easy, big boy," Jarrod told the horse brightly. "This will be over before you know it."

"Let's hope so," Cassie added as she got yanked back once more.

"I'm going to give him a tetanus shot and a penicillin shot. The rest of his vaccinations will have to wait a few days because I don't want to load him up with too much at once." He pulled the cap off one syringe and moved to the stallion's side. "Here we go."

After the horse reared up three times, kicked out twice, and circled at the end of the rope a half a dozen times, Jarrod finally got the one-second opportunity he needed to slip the needle into the stallion's neck. He gave his equine patient a quick pat before stepping away.

"There, that wasn't so bad, was it?" he announced.

Cassie glared at him while she gingerly flexed her shoulders. Her muscles ached already from trying to hold the stallion still, and Jarrod had a lot more to do. "It wasn't so bad for you, you mean. All you did was follow him around and dodge a couple kicks."

He grinned jauntily at her. "Exhausting work, all the same. How are you doing?"

"Great, just great." She pushed a lock of hair behind her ear. "You're on a roll. Give him the next one before he gets a chance to work up some more energy."

"The second shot should be a little easier," Jarrod said reassuringly, but the stallion proved him wrong. They went through an almost identical struggle when Jarrod attempted to get the needle into the opposite side of the horse's neck. If anything, the stallion fought harder.

"Good boy," Cassie praised the horse weakly as soon as the needle was removed.

"Well, let's see how he likes antiseptic washed through his cuts." Jarrod reached for the bottle and sponge he'd set aside. "Maybe he just has a strong aversion to shots."

The stallion kicked out again as Jarrod touched a soaked sponge to his lacerated chest.

"Maybe he just has a strong aversion to you," Cassie suggested.

"The things I'm doing to him don't exactly feel good, you know. I wouldn't be very pleasant about someone hurting me, either."

"You were right about one thing, though."

"What's that?"

"You said you didn't think it would go smoothly." She smiled sweetly. "You were right. It hasn't."

"It's nice to hear I was right about something." He let out a long, weary breath and stepped closer to the stallion again. "Back to work, fella. If you'd just let me get a couple good spongefuls of antiseptic down in there, I promise I'll leave you alone."

In the end, Jarrod had to settle for a few haphazard squirts. The stallion was getting himself too worked up to progress any further. Jarrod finished treating the last visible cut and tossed the sponge out of the way.

"You're through?" Cassie asked.

"For today. I'll leave you some antibiotics in tablet form that you can grind up and mix with his grain. That way, we don't have to go through the shots every day. Do you think you can wash out those lacerations twice a day from now on? A couple of them look like they're starting to get infected."

"I can do it if I have to." She gently scratched the stallion's neck. "It'll delay making friends with him, but I realize it has to be done."

"I'm still not thrilled about you working with him alone, but it would be pretty hard for me to get out here twice a day to help you."

"Don't worry, I can handle it. He probably won't act up as bad if you're not here."

"You let me know how it goes. I can try to work something out if you need my help."

"I'm sure that won't be necessary." At least, she hoped it wouldn't be. The whole time Jarrod had been here today, the memories of last night had lingered on the edge of her mind. She'd caught herself too often focusing on his mouth when he wasn't watching, or gazing appreciatively at the flex of his biceps while he struggled to treat her stallion. Only moments ago, she'd found herself staring in fascination at his tight buttocks while he bent over to tend to a cut on the horse's back leg.

She'd thought she was out of breath from the exertion of holding the stallion. Honestly assessing the situation now, she had to wonder if that was the true cause.

"You can put him back," Jarrod said.

She blinked up at him, ensnared in thoughts she had a difficult time eliminating. "What?"

"Killer. You can put him in his stall again."

"Oh." She turned the stallion around and led him away. Jarrod stepped in front of her to slide the door open. Her concentration still not entirely on the horse, Cassie wasn't prepared for him to bolt forward into the safety of his stall. The lead rope pulled out of her hand, burning as it went, while she stumbled suddenly out of balance. Strong, sure fingers gripped her arms and drew her close to a warm, iron-hard chest.

"Are you all right?" Jarrod asked, his own voice annoyingly husky. He'd been looking for an excuse to touch her again today, and the stallion had played along brilliantly. Only he hadn't been prepared for the blast of heat that coursed through him from simply holding her.

"Yes. I'm, uh, fine." Cassie's eyes flitted from Jarrod, to the horse, and then to her hands, which were already stinging from the rope burn. When Jarrod moved his hands off her arms and reached for her palms, she came to her senses and nearly jumped into the stall. The stallion had retreated to the far corner, but he didn't object to her coming up to him and unsnapping the lead rope. She left the stall immediately and closed the door behind her.

"That rope burn is going to hurt like hell in a little while," Jarrod told her.

It hurt like hell right now. "I'll be okay," she said with a shrug, steering her gaze away from him and onto the stallion. All at once, she remembered her plan to jar Jarrod's memory to see if he would associate her horse with Ebony Fire. "I sure wish I knew something about that horse's history," she began carefully.

Reluctantly, Jarrod switched his attention to the black stallion. "Yeah, I'll bet it would be a pretty interesting story."

"Especially the part that would tie in to why we both think he looks familiar."

He continued to study the horse, vaguely wondering why Cassie dwelled on the subject so much. "We'll figure it out someday."

She bit back her frustration when it appeared Jarrod didn't recognize Ebony Fire. "You still can't place him?" she probed.

"No." Something in her voice made his glance leave the horse to settle on her face. "Have you?"

"No," she lied. "Keep thinking about it, though, will you?"

"I'd rather think about his owner."

"Jarrod—"

"Sorry," he said, cutting her protest short. "I'll back off. How about dinner tomorrow night?"

Her eyebrows arched in faint amusement. "That's backing off?"

"Well, it all depends. If you want me to back off, then consider it another business meeting. However, if you're more daring, consider it a real date. And I promise, no beeper interruptions."

Daring? No, she'd call it more like total insanity. It would be something akin to emotional suicide to accept when the man aroused her senses so thoroughly. Still, it would present a good opportunity to discuss her stallion being Ebony Fire. At least that's what she told herself right before she agreed.

"Tomorrow night will be fine," she replied at last.

"Good." He started to head back to his truck. "Do you want to eat at the Club again?"

"How about if I make dinner for us here? I'd just as soon not run into Nathan Hall for a while."

His arm went around her shoulder and squeezed it playfully. "Just what I love. A cheap date."

"Ah, but I haven't said if this was business or pleasure, have I?"

Jarrod opened the door of his truck and sat down inside. "Call it whatever you want, Cassie. The pleasure's all mine either way."

She rolled her eyes and ignored the tingling tremors his words brought. "You've got quite a line on you, Doctor."

His grin stopped just short of being an obvious leer. "Wait until you see my bedside manner." He started the engine to prevent her from answering. "See you tomorrow night about six-thirty."

"You bet," she whispered as the exhaust fumes from his truck drifted away. If nothing else, tomorrow night would finally bring her the chance to tell Jarrod how wrong he'd been about her father. As she turned back to the barn, there was a bittersweet smile on her face.

Five

The stallion shifted nervously on his feet, then swung his back end around away from the leather-aproned man who was trying to get close enough to grab a hoof.

"I'm sorry, Larry," Cassie apologized to the man as he straightened up and sighed in exasperation. She knew she was pressuring the horse by attempting to get his feet trimmed by her farrier, but he needed to get some exercise. There was no way he could do that with his hooves in the condition they were in now.

"Move him over against the side of that stall," Larry instructed. "Make sure you don't stand right in front of him. I don't want him knocking you down if he tries to get away from me."

Cassie held the horse's head firmly with one hand and kept the other hand pushed against his chest to discourage him from moving forward. The stallion jerked his hind leg high in the air as Larry reached for it, but the farrier quickly grasped the foot and brought it down on his knee. He was able to get several good chunks of overgrown hoof trimmed off with his nippers before the horse pulled free again.

Larry stood up and wiped the sweat from his brow with his shirtsleeve. "I've trimmed worse-mannered horses before, Cassie," he grunted, "but not many."

She smiled reassuringly. "Think of the bright side. He's bound to get better."

The farrier snorted. "If I live long enough."

"Believe it or not, he isn't doing as bad as I thought he would. At least he's not really trying to kill you or anything."

"Thank God for small favors," Larry muttered. He patted the horse's hip. "Well, big fella, let's try and get that foot done one more time."

Cassie locked her attention on keeping the stallion as still as possible while Larry finished three of the hooves in brief stages. Only the horse's right rear remained untrimmed. Every time the farrier reached for that foot, the stallion would pin his ears and scuffle away.

"Easy, Bonfire," Cassie crooned soothingly as she tried to calm him. "Be a good boy now. You're almost all done."

"He's going to make a real fight out of this one, I'm afraid," Larry said. "I might have to tie up his left front leg to keep him from jumping around so much. Even then, I don't know that he'll let me get at that back foot."

"Do whatever you think is best, Larry."

He nodded. "I'll get my cotton rope."

In minutes, the stallion's left front leg was bent at the knee, the hoof touching his elbow, and tied securely with a soft cotton rope that ran around his pastern and up over his withers. To Cassie's immense relief, he didn't try to fight the rope at all.

"He's familiar with this little trick, I see," Larry commented. "So much the better. Maybe he'll behave himself now."

Behave wasn't quite the right word, Cassie thought to herself, but the stallion did allow Larry to speedily trim his last hoof after about ten minutes of wrestling around with it. She was amazed at the athletic prowess of the horse, who, while standing on only two legs, was still able to move his other back leg around almost at will and at the same time maintain his balance.

"You've got quite a horse there, Cassie," the farrier said as he released the stallion's front leg from its restraint. "Quite a horse indeed."

"Why, Larry," she teased, "I think you almost mean that as a compliment."

"Damned if I might, at that." He walked over to his truck and put his tools neatly away. "See you in a couple weeks."

"Right. And thanks a million."

"No problem." He waved out his window as he drove away.

Cassie led the stallion out to one of the empty white-railed corrals. She opened the gate and stepped inside with him. "All right, Bonfire, now that you can run around without hurting yourself on overgrown hooves, let's give you a chance to stretch out those long legs of yours." She unbuckled the lead rope from his halter and moved out of the way.

For a split second, the stallion froze. Then his muscles tensed, bunched, and exploded into action. With a flip of his head he was off, racing to the far side of the corral. Cassie backed out of the enclosure and shut the gate, her eyes never leaving the horse. He slid to a stop in the corner, one shoulder brushing against the sturdy rails. Nostrils flared and ears pricked forward, he whinnied a greeting to her other horses that were a hundred yards away in a pasture. Not waiting for a response, the stallion tucked his muzzle to his chest and galloped around the circumference of the corral, his tail held high like a billowing banner.

A lump rose in Cassie's throat as she watched him. It never ceased to move her seeing a horse run and play for the sheer pleasure of it. But witnessing this horse's exhilaration at his freedom, limited as it was, really choked her up. Was it because she was viewing the stunning gaits of Ebony Fire, a Thoroughbred who had once been called a future legend? Or was it simply because she was watching a magnificent animal regain a piece of joy after living through hell? She couldn't be sure, but she did know at that moment, she felt good, really good.

When the stallion stopped to catch his breath, she glanced at her watch. Four-thirty! Where had the afternoon gone? She only had two hours to get dinner ready before Jarrod arrived.

"Don't overdo yourself," she called to the horse. "I'll be back to get you in a little while. And you better not play hard to get, either!" She reluctantly pushed herself away from the corral and headed toward the house.

An hour later, she had spaghetti sauce simmering and a tossed salad thrown together. She straightened up the kitchen, set the table, put a frozen apple pie in the oven, and hurried back out to the barn to do her evening chores. Once all the other horses were fed except the black stallion, she hesitated in front of the corral he was in. She had a little less than half an hour to spare. Should she clean up and change first, then come back to catch the stallion, or put him away and change after that? Although if everything went well, she shouldn't get dirty simply catching a horse and feeding him, she still opted to clean up after the stallion was tucked in his stall for the night.

She ducked under one of the rails and walked into the corral. "Now don't you play games with me, Mister," she said, warningly shaking one finger at the horse. "I don't have time for it tonight." She approached him steadily head-on as he held his ground and watched her. When she was less than five feet away from him, he spun around and trotted off.

Cassie shrugged. Having him run away from her was far better than having him run *at* her. She'd definitely made progress with him these last few days. The satisfaction she felt over that was soon outweighed by frustration as six-thirty came ticking nearer and the stallion wouldn't let her get closer than three feet from him before he'd duck out of reach.

The sound of a car coming up her driveway was soon louder than her grumbled cursing. She glanced over her shoulder to see a silver Mercedes pulling to a stop by the house. The driver's door opened and Jarrod got out. She thought she could see the glint of his smile even from that distance as he waved and leaned against his car.

"I'll be right there," she yelled at him. Her voice dropped and she groaned. "Darn you, Bonfire! He's here and I look awful! Not to mention what kind of condition my spaghetti and pie are in by now." She took a deep breath and walked purposely toward the stallion. Large brown eyes shifted from Jarrod to her, and he stood there stock still, the picture of innocence. His ears flickered back as she reached up to grab his halter, but he didn't move away.

"Good boy!" she praised him, patting his neck. "If you would have done that ten minutes ago, you'd have been an even better boy. I swear you knew just what you were doing, didn't you?" She led him to the gate, snapped on the lead rope, and took him into the barn. Just as she was sliding his stall door shut, she heard a chuckle behind her.

"I hate to ask this—" Jarrod began.

"Then don't," she interrupted.

"How long have you been at that?"

She blew the damp bangs off her forehead and turned to face him. Her heart skipped a beat as she took in the vision of masculinity he portrayed. His long-sleeved white cotton shirt was pushed up to his elbows, revealing tanned and muscled forearms that had a sprinkling of dark hair over them. The black denim jeans that enfolded his lean lower body wouldn't be considered tight, she noted, but they couldn't have possibly fit any better. She steeled herself against the pesky flutters that rose in her stomach and realized he was waiting for an answer to something. What was it he'd asked her? Oh yes, about the horse.

"Actually, not quite a half an hour," she told him. "That's really pretty good, except I was hoping to have him put away before you got here."

"You got his feet trimmed today, huh?"

"Yes, and I couldn't wait to let him run around a little, even though it was so late by the time the farrier left."

She started walking out of the barn, and Jarrod fell into step at her side. "You could've taken a break to get ready and then tried to catch him again later," he pointed out casually.

The glance she gave him was mixed with surprise and curiosity. "You know as well as I do that once you start something with a horse, you have to see it through to the end or else they'll learn the wrong lesson. I couldn't leave that corral until I caught him."

"Yes, of course," he agreed thoughtfully. How many people did he know who would rather make a point with a horse than attend to their own appearance? Not many. Cassie could have avoided the situation entirely by postponing the stallion's exercise until tomorrow, but she cared too much about the beast's well-being. On second thought, maybe the choice hadn't been between the horse and what she looked like. Maybe it was between the horse and him. Maybe she didn't care one iota about impressing him. That would've certainly made it an easy choice for her. He frowned at that idea as they stepped up on the porch.

Cassie opened the front door and hurried off into the kitchen. After tending to the food, she walked back into the living room to find Jarrod standing in front of her aquarium.

"Can I get you something to drink?" she asked. "Dinner will be ready shortly, and I really have to take a quick shower."

"No, I'm fine right now. Nice tank."

"You should have seen it when it was full of saltwater fish," she said with a laugh as she moved past him into her bedroom. "I even had seahorses. But they're about the most difficult to keep, and it was too hard on me when they kept dying. I know they're only fish, but with that 'horse' in their name, well, it was just too much for me." She paused in the doorway with a somewhat embarrassed smile on her face. "So, I switched to tropicals. They're not as pretty, but they hang around longer. Anyway, I'll be out in a few minutes. Make yourself at home."

Jarrod's eyes stayed glued on her until the closed door hid her from his view. Suddenly, he had to sit down. Out of the blue, she'd shaken him, and he felt like he'd just been hit with a sledgehammer. What was he doing here with a woman whose emotions ran so deep and strong that she couldn't bear to keep seahorses because they died too frequently?

He sank into the softness of the couch and crossed his arms over his chest. *Take it easy, Fitzgerald,* he warned himself. She was just another beautiful woman, and he'd known plenty of those in his thirty-three years. He could handle it.

His gaze drifted back to the aquarium, which was easily the most dominating thing in the room. The tank had to be at least fifty gallons, and it was built into the middle of a wall-sized bookcase. Other than the couch, an easy chair, a television, and a stereo, there wasn't much else for furnishings. Still, it suited Cassie. Lovely, yet comfortable. Simple, and yet not so simple.

A quiet meow that came from near his feet made him jump. Jarrod grinned wryly to himself. He must be awfully tense for a cat to sneak up and startle him. He looked down at the petite long-haired white cat who was staring up at him with unwelcome, unblinking yellow eyes. When he reached down to pet it, the cat scampered out of the room. Would the feline's owner do the same if he tried to touch her, too? he wondered fleetingly.

He had no more time to ponder that thought as Cassie's bedroom door opened and she breezed back into the living room. Her long black hair was still wet in places from her shower, and she'd changed into clean blue jeans and a navy blouse. Did the color in her cheeks come from a compact or from his presence?

Cassie stopped in front of him and smiled. "Ready for a drink yet?" She hoped he wouldn't notice the breathless quality in her voice. Seeing him sitting so casually in her house was doing strange things to her nerves. Jarrod wasn't an overly large man, but the size of her room seemed to have shrunk immeasurably with him in it.

He shook his head. "I'll just wait for dinner."

"All right." She moved on to the kitchen. "I'll start the spaghetti and then we can eat."

Jarrod stood up and followed after her. He tucked his hands into his pockets and leaned against the door frame. "I met your roommate while you were in the shower."

"Roommate?" she repeated, momentarily puzzled. She finished filling a pan with water and put it on the stove. "Oh, you mean a cat?"

"Yeah."

She motioned for him to have a seat at the kitchen table. "Which one ventured forth?"

"A white one—"

"Sabrina," she supplied.

"You have more?"

"Two in the house. And any number of them around the barn. People are always dropping off strays here." She sat down across from him at the table. "I guess they figure since I take in unwanted horses, I should take in unwanted cats as well."

Jarrod picked up a salad fork and fingered the handle. "How did you get started rehabilitating horses?"

"I'd had it in the back of my mind for years. I went to quite a few lower-class auctions when I was still pretty young, and I always felt so sorry for the horses nobody wanted. I saw public displays of abuse everywhere around those sale barns." She shrugged, her eyes searching his. "I guess I planned on doing this kind of work later in life, af-

ter I'd been a trainer at a top-quality racing stable, and after I had saved enough money to be able to help more than
just a few. But, with the scandal over Ebony Fire's—'' she
hesitated ever so briefly ''—death, all of my plans got
changed whether I wanted them to or not.''

"Why?"

She gave him an exasperated look. "You know why. Have
you heard any good things about Mike Malone since Nate
fired him? Well, that distrust was relayed onto me. Don't
pretend you don't know that I'm on the Kentucky blue
blood blacklist.''

"Maybe I've heard a few things here and there, but I can't
believe not one single stable would take you on simply because of your father.''

"Believe it." She tossed her hair over her shoulder.
"There are even those who say I was the one responsible for
Ebony Fire's death, that my father took the blame to pro-
tect me.''

"Anyone who knew you at all would never believe such
a thing.''

Her eyes narrowed. "Anyone who knew my father
shouldn't have believed he was responsible, either. You
knew my father, Jarrod. That didn't stop you from believing the worst, did it?''

The tension between them was thick, even stifling. Jarrod took a deep breath and let it out slowly. "The facts were
undeniable.''

"The facts were fixed.''

"Cassie, it's not going to do us any good to keep rehash-
ing this issue. I've already told you I was sorry for what
happened to your father, and I'm sorry your career had to
suffer because of it.''

"The loss of my career stopped bothering me a long time
ago," she said frankly. "I love doing what I do, and I'm
probably happier with my life now than I would've been
working for someone else. I'll never be rich from this, but
it's extremely satisfying.''

"Maybe everything worked out for the best, then. You're doing work you find very rewarding."

Cassie rose and took the salad out of the refrigerator. She set it on the table and spooned out a bowl for him. "Speaking of rewarding work, how did you decide to become a vet?"

He waited until she had her own bowl filled with lettuce before answering. "My father wanted me to be a doctor."

She paused with her fork midway to her mouth and stared blankly at him. "I don't get it."

"Get what?"

"You mean your father wanted you to be a medical doctor, as in a human doctor?"

"That's right."

"So..." she drawled leadingly.

"So, I was just rebellious enough not to do exactly what he wanted. I decided to heal horses instead of people."

"And what did your father think of that?"

"At first, he wasn't very pleased." He smiled sardonically. "Then later, once he got used to the idea, I think he felt it wasn't such a bad career move for me after all. He has a stable full of horses, you know, and it comes in handy having a son who's a vet. It turned out quite practical for him."

Cassie put her fork down and studied him candidly. "Your little revolt didn't work out, then."

"No, I wouldn't say that. I'm probably a lot better suited to be a vet than a medical doctor."

"I suppose so," she agreed smoothly. "You couldn't get away with being so aloof with your patients if they were human." She got up quickly, chagrined at her hasty words, and pulled the cooked spaghetti off the stove.

"You think I'm aloof with my patients?"

She lifted one shoulder, glad her back was to him. "I think you have the same attitude about them as most of their owners do."

"Horse racing is big business, you know that. Besides, I'd never survive if I got personally involved with all the horses I treat."

"Perhaps," she acknowledged as she emptied the spaghetti into a serving dish. "But I think it would be nice if you got involved enough to know one of your patients from another."

"Meaning?"

"Oh, I don't know." Unable to think of anything else to detain her, she returned to the table with their dinner. "I guess I'm trying to piece together the puzzle about my black stallion. I was thinking earlier about what black Thoroughbred we might both have known. Ebony Fire was one possibility I came up with."

Something in her tone held his attention on her face more than her words. "But Ebony Fire is dead," he reminded her flatly. "That kind of leaves him out of the running, wouldn't you say?"

"Maybe." She took a deep breath, hoping to somehow draw in some extra courage along with the oxygen. "And then again, maybe not."

In a flash of movement, Jarrod reached over and grabbed her wrist. He held it tightly until she looked at him. Her clear blue eyes told him what he wanted to know, but he asked anyway. "What are you saying?"

"I'm saying my stallion strongly resembles Ebony Fire." She watched while disbelief and shock crossed through him, only to be replaced by slow acknowledgement. Her heart started hammering against her ribs, and she did her best to ignore the jolt of awareness that crept up her arm at his touch. "You think so, too, don't you?"

He released her and sat back in the chair. His memory of Nate's champion horse wasn't especially sharp, but it was good enough for him to realize she had a point. "All right, so maybe your rogue does look like Ebony Fire, but what difference does that make? He can't *be* Ebony Fire."

"Are you sure about that?"

"Of course, I'm sure. I checked over the autopsy on Ebony Fire myself."

"You checked over an autopsy that was done on a black horse. I think it's pretty coincidental you were out of town when Ebony Fire supposedly died. I think Nate planned it that way so you wouldn't be the one to perform the autopsy. He couldn't take the chance on you examining the dead horse too carefully."

"That's absurd," Jarrod scoffed. "I can't imagine Nate doing such a thing. You are insinuating he pulled off some kind of scam, aren't you?"

"That's exactly what I'm insinuating. And I have no doubts about what a dirty player Nate can be in any game. He could have done it."

"But why would he? Ebony Fire was in his prime. He had all the rich three-year-old races ahead of him, and maybe another year or two of racing after that. Then there would be his value at stud. Nate couldn't have possibly made more off an insurance policy than the horse would have been worth alive."

"Don't think I haven't considered all of that," she admitted. "But when I look at that stallion in my barn, I know I'm right."

Jarrod shook his head impatiently. "It's crazy."

"I know."

"It's impossible."

"That," she said, "I don't know."

He'd heard enough. If he didn't steer her away from this line of thinking, he knew they'd only end up arguing. Not only that, but he'd come here to have a pleasant evening with a beautiful woman, not to have his head spinning from some farfetched theory.

Jarrod gave her a relaxed grin. "The spaghetti is going to get cold if we don't get started eating. It looks and smells far too good to let that happen. Why don't we eat now and continue this discussion another time?"

His easy charm was almost persuasive enough to chase away all thoughts of horses and scandals from her mind. Almost. She started to serve the food, but she wasn't quite ready to completely abandon their conversation.

"Jarrod?"

"Yes?"

"Are you a betting man?"

One eyebrow jutted up in amusement. "I've been known to be on occasion. Why?"

She handed him a heaping plate of steaming spaghetti. As soon as he'd set it down, she firmly and deliberately placed her hand over his. When he glanced up in surprise, she smiled. "Then you can bet on this. I will find out what really happened to Ebony Fire three years ago. You can choose to help me or hinder me or do neither, but I will find out. And that's a promise."

Jarrod's eyes lingered on her face long after she'd removed her hand and started to eat. Passion. The lady was full of it. Maybe not entirely for him, he admitted grudgingly to himself, but for life and her causes. He'd long since given up on finding a special woman to spend his future with. Content with things the way they were, Jarrod was in no way looking for any complications. He supposed that was why he'd started to discover that the more time he spent with Cassie, the more uneasy he became. Yet for a moment, he allowed no fear, no tenseness, to cloud and unnerve him. This time, he didn't fight the excitement that surged through him just being around her. Instead, he reveled in it.

Almost mechanically, he brought a bite of spaghetti into his mouth, scarcely noticing that he didn't even taste it. He could have laughed out loud at his own foolishness. He'd thought her theories about Ebony Fire had caused his head to spin? Well, the joke was on him. He was thinking about nothing but her now, and his head was spinning as fast as a spiraling carnival ride.

As she worked at cleaning up her plate, Cassie wasn't sure whether to be pleased or disappointed at Jarrod's reaction. At least her speculations about Ebony Fire were out in the open. Would he give the matter serious thought? She hoped so, for she knew she could use his help in exposing the whole thing. Nate was a wealthy and powerful man, and . . .

She almost choked on her food. Nate was also one of Jarrod's best clients. Where would Jarrod's true loyalty lie? With her or with Nate? Maybe she should have kept her mouth shut about the entire business. Maybe Jarrod would even warn Nate. Maybe—

"What's going through that creative little mind of yours now?" Jarrod asked.

She swallowed guiltily and slowly raised her gaze to his face. Curious gray eyes met hers openly, with just a hint of concern. At once, she felt her agitation subside slightly. She could sense the decency that was a part of Jarrod. He wouldn't protect wrong over right, deceit over honor.

She made a pretense of looking offended. "I beg your pardon. I don't have a little mind."

"All right, scratch the little. You won't argue with the creative part, will you?"

"I guess not."

"Fine. So what were you just thinking about?"

"I was thinking it was about time to dish out the dessert." She stood up and carried her plate to the sink. "Do you want a piece of apple pie?"

Jarrod pushed his chair back and rose to his feet. He set his dishes down next to hers on the counter. One hand leisurely lifted a strand of her hair that had fallen forward and put it back over her shoulder. "Sure," he murmured.

She trembled before she could get control of herself. "Jarrod—"

"Why won't you tell me what was really going through your mind a minute ago?"

"All right, I will," she said, her voice cool. She was furious with herself for reacting to the slightest touches from him. "I was thinking about whether it was wise for me to tell you what I think happened to Ebony Fire. I was thinking that you are probably real close to Nathan Hall and that I probably shouldn't trust you. I was thinking—"

"You're doing far too much thinking," Jarrod interrupted. He took hold of both her arms and turned her so that her back was against the sink. He stepped in front of her, switching his hands from her arms to the counter on either side of her. He watched the pulse on the side of her neck quicken and realized his own was beating maddeningly fast. "Forget what you think. Tell me what you feel."

"I feel..." She started the sentence, but could think of no way to finish it. Anger instantly dissipated into something much warmer and even more disarming. Every muscle in her body was threatening to give out at his commanding nearness, but she had nothing to grab onto for support except him. Her fingers twitched with the desire to trace over the broad muscular chest that was only inches away.

His head lowered further until his lips were just a breath from hers. "Yes? Go on."

Go on with what? she wondered absently. Her mind refused to function properly as her senses were flooded with awareness. The first reaction she felt when his mouth covered hers was relief that she could stop trying to come up with an answer. Her second reaction was one of awe. How could the simple act of lips meeting lips be so incredible, so explosive, so arousing? Her hands moved on their own accord to join around his neck and pull him closer still. With very little pressure, his mouth urged hers open, and his tongue darted inside to entice and intoxicate.

As his tongue continued to purposefully explore the contours of her mouth, she gasped at the jolt of longing that ripped through her. Every nerve ending tingled; every skin cell cried out for direct contact with his hard body. She was drowning in a pool of sensations and yearnings that had such a strong current she could barely get enough air into her lungs to breathe. It was then she suddenly froze in fear, as the feeling of slipping away from everything logical and reasonable and sane became too overpowering to ignore.

Her hands shifted to push against his chest as she jerked her mouth away. She didn't have enough strength left to shove him very far, but she succeeded in getting her point across even though there wasn't much space separating them.

With an effort, Jarrod unfolded his fingers from the edge of the counter. His knuckles were white and stiff from keeping his hands on the Formica instead of moving to any part of Cassie's body. Desire had taken hold of him that intensely.

He took a deep breath, hoping to calm his raging bloodstream. It wasn't that easy. He let go of the counter and took a step backward. "How about some of that apple pie?" he suggested unevenly. He was too tied up in knots to even smile as he said it.

"Apple pie," she mumbled. "Right." She turned and pulled a knife out of the silverware drawer. Her hands were shaking so badly she could hardly hold it.

"Cassie, this is ridiculous," Jarrod burst out. "We can't just go on with the evening and pretend this never happened."

"You're the one who said you wanted pie."

"What I really want is you, and you know it."

Yes, she knew it all right. What she didn't know was how to deal with it. Or how to deal with herself. "It's important we maintain a good professional relationship," she said weakly.

His laugh was short and held a touch of sarcasm. "Don't tell me you won't admit we crossed the line from business to pleasure a long time ago."

"Maybe we shouldn't have," she whispered.

"Maybe we couldn't have prevented it even if we wanted to." He reached out to gently cup her shoulder. "What we need to decide is where we're going to go from here."

For a moment, she swayed into his hand, then quickly twisted away. "Don't," she warned.

"Don't what?"

"Don't touch me again tonight. I don't think I can handle it." She set the knife onto the counter and faced him. "In fact, maybe you should just leave now."

He searched her velvety blue eyes for a sign of irritation or hostility, but saw only a soft pleading for understanding. "If that's what you really want," he said slowly.

She nodded, even though her body was trying to persuade her otherwise. She positively ached to finish what they'd so briefly started. "Stop by tomorrow, if you have time. Maybe I'll have had a chance to check my stallion's lip tattoo by then."

The damn horse. How could she think about that rogue right now? It annoyed him enough to make him forget to tell her to be careful. "I'll make the time. Thanks for dinner." He started to walk out of the kitchen but stopped when he realized she wasn't following. "Aren't you going to show me to the door?"

She overlooked the challenge in his voice and shook her head. "I don't think so."

He grinned. He'd really gotten to her tonight. Even though she was kicking him out early, he felt tremendous satisfaction in knowing she was as unnerved by the attraction between them as he was. "Coward," he retorted cheerfully.

She smiled at that. "Hardly. I just know when to not press my luck."

"I hope next time you'll press it a little further." He ducked out of the kitchen. "See you tomorrow," he called, right before the front door shut behind him.

As Jarrod started up his car, he made a silent vow. Soon, very soon, he'd make sure Cassie would indeed press her luck to the limit. He wouldn't listen to that little voice inside him that said if he had a lick of sense, he'd run the other way and never look back. He was in too deep already to do that. He was probably in over his head, in fact.

"What the hell," he muttered aloud.

He'd been simply treading water for years now. It was time to find out whether he was meant to sink or swim.

Six

"Thoroughbred Registry, Meg speaking. Can I help you?"

Cassie swallowed nervously and cleared her throat. "Yes, I hope so. I have a registration number I'd like verified as being correct."

"Sure, no problem. What's the number?"

Cassie stared at the scratch paper where ten minutes earlier she'd scribbled down her black stallion's tattoo number. What if she was wrong about Ebony Fire? What if she wasn't able to clear her father's name after all? So much of her theory rode on this six-digit number.

She took a deep breath and picked up the scratch paper. "Two-one-seven-eight-six-four," she said at last.

"Okay, hold on a moment while the computer checks this out. It'll only take a second— oh, here we go. That number belongs to a five-year-old stallion bred in Maryland named Finish First."

Cassie felt her heart drop all the way to her toes. "Are you sure?"

"No doubt about it. Anything else?"

"What color is he?"

"Says here he's black with a white star and a white sock on his right rear leg."

"Can you tell me who his current owner is?"

"Peter Erickson in Kentucky."

Cassie closed her eyes briefly. "Thanks," she murmured, and hung up the phone.

That was it, then. The stallion in her barn was Finish First, not Ebony Fire. She crushed the scratch paper into a tiny ball and threw it across the room. She'd been so sure she was right. Or had she been looking so hard for a way to vindicate her father that she'd simply let her imagination run wild?

Feeling gloomy and morose, she walked outside. A warm, captivating breeze lifted the hair from around her face as she slowly inhaled the fresh air. Without conscious thought, she wandered over to the corral where she'd let the stallion loose after she'd read his lip tattoo. She crossed her arms over the top rail and watched him alternate between trotting and grazing.

"You are Ebony Fire," Cassie told the horse. "You have to be."

But the evidence now was overwhelming in favor of her being wrong. She would have to face up to that and learn to live with it. And she would have to find another way to clear Mike Malone's name.

Cassie was so caught up in her thoughts, she didn't hear Jarrod's truck drive in until he was almost right up to the barn. A weak smile was the only greeting she offered him as he approached.

"What's wrong?" he asked immediately.

She flinched inwardly and bit down on her lower lip. Was she that transparent? Her gaze returned to the stallion, who was intently staring at Jarrod from the other end of the corral. "What do you mean?"

"You look like you just lost your best friend." Jarrod scrutinized her from head to toe, but she seemed to be all right physically. More than all right, as usual. But something was definitely bothering her. Deflated. That's what she looked like, he decided. "Did something happen to one of your horses?"

"No, they're all fine, and so am I."

"I don't think so."

"Well, I do." She turned toward him, and was momentarily startled by the concern in his eyes. "You're imagining something that isn't there."

"Am I?"

"Yes." *Tell him,* an inner voice urged. *Tell him and get it over with.* Her mouth opened, but the words wouldn't come. She'd have to wait until another time to expose her theory as mere wishful thinking.

"Cassie, what is it?"

She felt his hand on her back and immediately sidestepped away from the contact. "It's nothing. Will you please just forget it?"

He knew he wasn't getting anywhere, but it was hard to back off. It was harder still to refrain from touching her again. Her lips were set unyieldingly together right now, but he'd be willing to bet he could get them to soften and part with very little coercion from his own. It took substantial work to switch his thoughts and the conversation around.

"I was thinking about your speculations today when I was at Nate's place," he replied casually, "and I got a little information for you that might prove helpful."

Cassie released a heavy sigh. What little satisfaction she got from hearing that Jarrod had actually considered her ideas was quickly overshadowed by dread. Irritation was soon to follow. When had she started caring so much about what he thought of her that she couldn't admit to being a fool?

"What kind of information?" she finally asked.

"I saw an old photo layout they'd made up for when Ebony Fire was going to be eventually syndicated for breeding, and it had his registration number on it. I copied it down for you." He pulled a scrap of paper from his pocket and held it out to her.

"Thanks," she mumbled as she took it from him.

He waited for her to at least look at it, but she didn't. She merely held it loosely in her hand as if she wouldn't care one iota if the wind stripped it from her grasp.

"I realize it's not exactly classified information," Jarrod remarked, "but I thought you'd be a little more interested in it."

"I am interested, it's just that I've got other things on my mind today." Out of a sense of obligation, she glanced down at the paper. Her attention was already back on the stallion when the numbers sank in. She did a double take and re-read the registration number again.

It was close, very close to the number she'd been given today for the horse named Finish First. She'd have to retrieve her notation to be sure.

"I'll be right back," she called over her shoulder as she sprinted to the house.

She found the crumpled up wad of paper and carefully unfolded it. The numbers were identical except for two of the digits. She hurried back out to Jarrod, her pulse in triple-time, her mind in a whirl.

"What's going on?" Jarrod demanded.

"Look at this." She thrust the two pieces of paper in front of him. "This is the number you just gave me. The other one is the number I got off my stallion today. I called—"

"Wait a minute," Jarrod cut in. "You got his tattoo number today?"

"Well, yes, I did."

"Why didn't you tell me?"

She shrugged one shoulder. "That doesn't matter now. The important thing is, I called the Registry right before you got here. They told me the number I got off my stallion belongs to a five-year-old Thoroughbred named Finish First, whose last registered owner is Pete Erickson.''

Jarrod frowned. "He's the one the humane organization took that rogue away from, isn't he?"

"Yes," she said jubilantly.

"So what are you so excited about? It sounds like Finish First is the horse in that corral. It couldn't be Ebony Fire."

"That's what I thought at first, too, until you gave me Ebony Fire's registration number. Oh, Jarrod, don't you see?"

"No, I guess I don't."

"Look at the numbers. Ebony Fire's is two-one-seven-three-six-one. There are only two digits different from Finish First's."

"So?"

"The two numbers that are different are the 'three' and the last 'one.' Those two numbers could have been altered into an 'eight' and a 'four,' so they'd match Finish First's registration number." She took a deep breath. "It was Finish First who died in Nate's stable. Ebony Fire lived on with Finish First's identity."

Jarrod groaned. "Cassie, come on. That's pretty damn farfetched, don't you think?"

"It could have been done," she insisted. "It's too coincidental that those two horses were both black and their registration numbers were so close. Nate must've done a lot of research before he pulled this off. He was awfully lucky to find another horse who could be switched with Ebony Fire so easily."

"Did Ebony Fire have a white hind sock?"

She hesitated a moment before answering. "No, he didn't."

"There, how do you explain that?" Jarrod proclaimed. "You don't expect me to believe Nate changed the tattoo and painted Ebony Fire's back leg white, do you?"

"No, of course not," she said impatiently, "but it could've been done another way."

"How?"

"I don't know how, but Nate must have."

Jarrod shook his head. "Okay, even if all of this is physically possible, which I'm not convinced of for a second, that still brings us back to one big problem with your theory."

"What's that?"

"Why?" he said simply. "Why would Nate do all this?"

"I don't know that yet, but—"

"I mean, if he wanted to collect the insurance money on Ebony Fire for some reason, why kill another horse and perform a switch in identities? He'd be taking a pretty big risk of getting caught. Why would Nate do anything that stupid?"

"Maybe greed," she suggested. "Nate always struck me as a man who likes to live dangerously. Maybe he wanted to recoup what he paid for Finish First as well as collect the insurance money."

"Possibly, but we still have no idea why Nate would collect on the insurance policy instead of letting Ebony Fire go on with his racing career and stand at stud."

Cassie grinned at his choice of words. "We?"

"Did I say that? A mere slip of the tongue."

Her smile didn't diminish as she placed her hand on his upper arm. "You think I could be right, don't you?"

"No way," he snorted.

"And you're going to help me, aren't you?"

He stared down at her and felt his usual common sense get completely lost and disappear in the depths of her violet blue eyes. "I might," he offered playfully, "if the incentive is appealing enough."

"Incentive?"

"Yeah, incentive."

She blinked, feigning innocence. "You mean exposing a cruel, dishonest man and clearing the name of a wonderful, innocent one isn't enough incentive?"

He laughed and pulled her into his arms. "Sorry, that's not even close."

"Then you're not even close to the kind of man I thought you were."

"Oh, really? Then I am making progress. The first day I drove up to your farm, you thought I was something just short of an ogre."

Her gaze rested involuntarily on his full mouth, a mouth that was capable of bringing her incomparable pleasure. She dragged her eyes up to meet his. "I guess you just confirmed that impression was the most accurate," she said smartly.

"I guess I need to convince you otherwise again."

Jarrod's lips lowered to gently caress her forehead, nose, cheeks, and chin. They roamed everywhere on her face, except for the one place he knew would provide the most explosive sensations. He deftly avoided that contact until he felt the tension build inside her. His mouth ceased its seductive teasing then, and honed in to fuse with hers.

As his lips molded and moved against her own, a tiny moan escaped from Cassie's throat. Fire had ignited at once, and her body was engulfed with intense liquid heat. Hunger was unleashed, need unfurled. His tongue probed, met hers, and continued to plunder. The intensity of the rapture he elicited was as welcome as it was startling.

Just when she thought his mouth had brought her all the pleasure she could handle, Cassie felt the light brushing of his knuckles against the tip of one of her already peaked nipples. All the remaining air in her lungs deserted her as thousands of shock waves rippled through her body. Jarrod's hand rotated so the palm covered her breast and gently massaged the sensitized flesh still covered by her T-shirt and bra. She trembled from a longing sharp enough to be almost painful.

A shrill, piercing whinny from the stallion in the corral was loud enough to break through the passion-induced fog clouding Cassie's brain. She started badly, simultaneously breaking her mouth free and pushing Jarrod's hand away. Turning her head to glance at the horse, she noticed his attention was focused on a group of horses that had wandered close to his paddock.

Jarrod felt her withdraw away from him even though he still held her close with one arm. What would it take to bring her back to him? he wondered. "That horse has the worst timing," he muttered, softly kissing her temple.

"Jarrod, I—" she began.

"No. Forget about him, forget about everything except how we feel when we're together. Think about how much more we could feel."

"I can't." She ducked under his arm and took a step backward. Twisting her hands, she stared out at the distant rolling bluegrass hills. "I don't understand how it happens, but my body takes over for my mind when I'm with you. However, I'm not about to let it rule me completely. As much as I hate to admit it, I need you as a vet. I don't want to take a chance on ruining our professional relationship."

"Life is full of nothing but chances, Cassie. You can't run away from all of them." With one finger, he drew a line down the length of her arm. "I just think you should leave your mind open to some very interesting and fulfilling possibilities."

The corner of her mouth curved upwards in a smirk. "Like finding out and proving what really happened to Ebony Fire?"

"That's not what I meant, and you know it."

"Maybe, but it's a good place to start."

"Knowing you, it's probably the only place to start."

She had to smile. "You're learning, Jarrod."

"I'll give you fair warning, Miss Malone," he said, his silvery eyes bright and full of promise. "I plan on learning a whole lot more."

Despite her strictest resolve, a tremor of anticipation went through her. She squelched it as best she could. There were more important things for her to think about. Her mind must remain clear and centered on exposing Nathan Hall. She owed it to her father, and she owed it to herself.

And she owed it to a poor black Thoroughbred named Finish First.

Jarrod slowly approached his best client, undecided even now whether to bring up the subject that had been nagging him for twenty-four hours. Nathan Hall did not appear to be in the best of moods today. Jarrod halted in the shadows for a moment, watching Nate bawl out a young groom.

As he studied Nate unobtrusively, Jarrod's mind drifted back to his conversation with Cassie yesterday. How many times this morning had he wondered if there was even the slimmest chance she could be right in her suspicions? The whole thing was so damned implausible. He only wished the events surrounding Ebony Fire's death had remained clearer in his memory. All he could draw on was the stalwart belief that Cassie's father had been directly responsible for the racehorse's demise. The facts that had led him to the conclusion had seemed irrefutable at the time, and yet . . .

"Jarrod!" Nate called out. "I didn't see you standing there. All through with your rounds here already?"

"Yes." Pulling out a smile from somewhere, Jarrod stepped forward. "Storm Cloud and Visions of Glory are both coming along nicely. Storm Cloud should be ready to train again in a few days, but I'd give Visions of Glory at least another week to rest up."

"Whatever you say. Your instructions are law around here. Have you spoken to my trainer?"

He nodded. "I just got through talking to him."

"Good." Nate turned and gave Jarrod a curious glance. "Have you been seeing much of Cassandra Malone lately?"

Jarrod swallowed down his surprise. Here he'd been trying to think of a way to bring up the subject, and Nate had done it for him. "A little. Why?"

"Oh, no reason. I just find the two of you to be a rather, shall we say, unlikely couple."

"I find her as fascinating as she is beautiful, and the work she does with some of those horses is truly remarkable. In fact, she just got a black Thoroughbred stallion about a week ago, and she's made unbelievable progress with him already."

"Is that so?" Nate reached out to pat the nose of one of his horses, seemingly uninterested.

Jarrod chuckled nonchalantly, but his eyes were glued on Nate's face. "That horse was in pretty bad shape when she got him. Some bozo named Pete Erickson had abused him something terrible."

"Men like him are a disgrace to the good name of racing," Nate commented coolly.

"You know him?"

"I've seen him around."

"Yeah, well, after talking to Cassie, I've come to realize there are a lot of rather unscrupulous racehorse owners around. Men and women who would do anything for a buck."

Nate's answering smile was slow and smooth. "Some people take their business very seriously, Jarrod."

"I guess so." He couldn't think of anywhere else to take the conversation, so he had no choice but to make his departure. With a final shake of his head, he turned away. "I've got a lot of clients to take care of yet today. See you tomorrow."

As Jarrod headed back to his truck, he shook his head in disgust. What had he been trying to prove, anyway? He'd known Nate for a lot of years and he'd barely known Mike Malone. Evidence was evidence. Mike Malone had been solely responsible for Ebony Fire's death. So why had he been attempting to trap Nate into slipping up by reacting to the news of Cassie's stallion?

Who would've thought he'd ever let a pretty face distort his thinking? But then, Cassie was more than just another beautiful lady. That, of course, was the crux of his problem.

Jarrod had long ago come to terms with living his life virtually alone. For years, playing the field with rather remote detachment had been fairly satisfying. So why was the thought of other women suddenly so unappealing? And the thought of Cassie so all consuming? When he thought about her spunk, her passion, her intelligence, and yes, her body, he only knew he had to have her.

As he pulled to a halt behind a stop sign, a wry smile claimed Jarrod's features. There was one little snag in his plan. Cassie. So far, he hadn't had much success in convincing her to let their relationship progress. Her mind was centered on accomplishing a single goal—clearing her father's name. Before he could get anywhere with her, she would have to release the bitterness of a past that still haunted her day and night. It was up to him to help her.

There was really only one way to do that. He'd continue to spend time with her in the guise of proving Ebony Fire was still alive. Then, when the moment came that she had to face up to being wrong, he'd be right there to see her through it. And beyond.

Seven

"This has to be the slowest Friday night I've ever worked," Denise groaned.

"I won't argue with you there," Cassie agreed as she filled up a glass of water for herself from the sink in the kitchen. Friday nights at the Country Club were almost without exception the busiest of the week. Someone must have forgotten to inform all their usual customers of that fact tonight, she mused. The place had been dead all evening.

"You haven't told me how things are going with Jarrod."

Cassie took a sip of water. "You haven't asked."

"That's because I was hoping you'd volunteer the information. You weren't so closemouthed about your last boyfriend."

"Jarrod isn't my boyfriend."

"Oh?" Denise looked far from convinced. "What would you call him, then?"

"I'd call him my vet. Nothing more."

Denise shook her head and laughed. "I don't know why you're fighting it so much, Cass. Is he as good a kisser as he looks like he'd be?"

"Better," she said with a sigh, then flushed with embarrassment. "You sure set me up for that one, didn't you?"

"I just hope I get all the juicy details when you're comfortable enough to talk about him. I've had fantasies about that man for years."

Cassie gave her a playful push toward the door. "Get out there and take care of your three customers and forget about Jarrod and me."

"Okay, okay." Denise pushed open the swinging door, only to stop in mid-stride. "Oh, Cass?"

"What?"

"Your vet is here. And guess what? He just sat down in your section. Want to trade?"

"I don't care," Cassie said indifferently, but she couldn't quite pull it off.

"Liar." Denise winked. "He's all yours, honey. I only hope you're smart enough to know what to do with him."

The towel Cassie threw at Denise's head hit the back of the door instead. She took a moment to gather her composure before walking out into the dining room.

"Hungry, Doctor?"

Jarrod turned toward the familiar, slightly throaty voice. "What a question," he murmured as his eyes trailed down the length of her. There wasn't another waitress here who filled that uniform so perfectly.

"Let me rephrase that." She let out her breath when she realized she'd been holding it. Why wasn't she irritated instead of thrilled he was staring at her so brazenly? "What can I get for you?"

"I'm afraid that question isn't any better, Cassie." He glanced down at her long, shapely legs before lifting his eyes to hers. "Do you really want me to answer that honestly?"

"That's all right, I'll just use my imagination. Do you want something to eat or not?"

He couldn't help grinning. "Just coffee, please."

"You came all the way to the Club for coffee?"

"Of course not. I came to see you."

Her heart skipped a beat, perhaps to gather strength to race at the crazy speed it was now doing. She'd never need to take up aerobics as long as Jarrod was around. He gave her heart all the exercise it could handle. "What do you want to see me about?"

"Nothing important," he said lightly. "It can wait until you're done with your shift."

"I get off at midnight."

Jarrod looked around the mostly deserted dining room. "I'll bet you could leave now if you asked. They could certainly get along without you for the rest of the night."

"Maybe." She hated to lose the money by taking off early, but with so few customers, she wouldn't make much in tips anyway. And Jarrod did have her curiosity piqued. "I'll go check."

Minutes later she'd retrieved her coat and purse and was standing in the parking lot with Jarrod. The cool night air breezed against her heated skin, but did nothing to lower her inner body temperature.

"So where do you want to go?" she asked.

"It doesn't matter. We can stop somewhere for a drink, if you like."

Cassie held out her arms. "Dressed like this? I don't think so."

"We can just go back to your place, then."

She swallowed nervously, remembering all too well what had happened the last two times he'd been at her house. Each time she'd lost a little more control, ached for him with a stronger intensity. How many more times could she tempt herself like that?

"Okay. I'll meet you there." She climbed into her car and roared away before her practical, sensible side could convince her of the foolhardiness of that decision.

* * *

Cassie was leading the way up her driveway when she saw it. If her eyes didn't always instinctively go to the barn upon returning home, she might have never noticed. Bypassing the garage, she screeched to a stop in front of the barn. She was already sliding open the doors by the time Jarrod was getting out of his truck.

"Is this a normal routine for you, or is something wrong?" he called to her from the doorway.

Cassie didn't break stride in her quick check of all the horses. The black stallion was the only one in an agitated state, which somehow didn't surprise her. "Didn't you see it?"

"See what?"

"There was a light on in the barn. Just as we were driving up, it went off." Her gaze flew over every inch of the barn again. "Someone was in my barn."

"Why would someone be in your barn?"

"I have no idea. Unless..." She looked at her stallion, who was still pacing anxiously around the confines of his stall. "Maybe someone was trying to get at Ebony Fire."

"Maybe you just imagined it," he suggested. "Maybe you only saw the outside light."

"No way. It came from inside the barn." She ran to one corner and dragged out a stepladder.

"What are you doing now?"

"I'm going to prove to you that these lights were on when we drove up." She spread out the legs of the ladder underneath a light bulb that was wired to an overhead beam. She'd already scrambled up two rungs when she felt a hand around her ankle.

"Calm down. You're going to hurt yourself in the condition you're in."

"I have to see if the light bulbs are hot. They wouldn't be yet from the amount of time I've had them on."

Jarrod shook his head. "You're quick, I'll give you that. Quick and clever. And upset. Let me go up the ladder."

"I'm quite capable of checking a light bulb myself." She glared down at the hand that was still holding her ankle captive. "Who do you think changes them when they burn out?"

He reluctantly released her and firmly grabbed the ladder. "Fine. Go on up yourself. Just take it easy, okay?"

Finally unimpeded, she hurried up the rungs until she was level with the bulb. One index finger reached out and touched the white exterior, only to jerk instantly away. It was burning hot.

"I knew it!" she declared jubilantly. In seconds she was back on the floor next to him. She nodded toward the bulb. "Go see for yourself."

"I assume it's hot?"

"I almost scorched my finger on it."

"Cassie, light bulbs do heat up pretty fast, you know."

"Not that fast. Go on up yourself if you don't believe me."

"I'll take your word for it." He was smiling at her despite her seriousness with the situation. The lady was like a little tornado. She was a bundle of energy in everything she did. At that moment, he wanted more than anything to feel her passionate energy directed at him in bed.

"It had to be Nate, you know."

"What?" It was difficult to redirect his thoughts. He'd much rather dwell on making love to her than on her perceived view of Nathan Hall's treachery.

"Nate must have tracked down Ebony Fire somehow. Maybe he talked to Pete Erickson or something. Still, it wouldn't have been easy to trace him to me. All those records are confidential."

Jarrod cleared his throat. "Maybe he found out another way."

Her attention was at once riveted on him. "How?"

"Yesterday when I was at Nate's, I sort of hinted around about the new black stallion you'd taken in."

"You *what? Jarrod, how could you!"

"Well, I wanted to catch him in some kind of reaction. It was a test. I did it to help you."

"It's not going to help me when Nate gets rid of the best piece of evidence there is against him! Maybe he was trying to steal Ebony Fire tonight. You know what that horse's fate would be if Nate got a hold of him again."

"Assuming you're right about everything."

Cassie groaned in frustration. "Oh, please. How much more proof do you need? Do you think it was mere coincidence that someone was in my barn the day after you told Nate about my stallion? The only reason he probably didn't come out right away yesterday was because I would have been here. Nate knows I work Friday nights. If I hadn't come home early tonight, Ebony Fire might be dead right now."

Once again, the tiniest edge of doubt crept into Jarrod's mind. He squashed it immediately. Cassie had to be over-reacting. Still, he couldn't pass up such a golden opportunity. "I don't think you should stay here alone for a while."

"That's ridiculous," she scoffed. "I'll be fine. However, I'm going to have to take Ebony Fire somewhere else. I can't take a chance on his safety."

"Oh, that's great. Look after the horse and make sure he's all right, but just forget about yourself."

Cassie ignored his sarcasm. "I know Nate is capable of many things, but I don't think that would include harming me."

"If you're right about all of this, then Nate has millions of dollars at stake, as well as his whole career. He could even be facing a lengthy jail term. You're not his favorite person in the world anyway. Why would he think twice about disposing of you?"

"You should've thought about that before you told him I had Ebony Fire."

Jarrod jammed his hands into his pockets. "I was still fighting the idea that Nate could be guilty."

"So what was his reaction?"

"Nothing, absolutely nothing. There was no surprise, no show of nerves, no expression of dread. He acted like the news didn't matter to him at all."

"As much as you seem to want Nate to be innocent, I doubt you'd notice any reaction unless it was very obvious." Cassie folded up the ladder and carried it back to the corner. "That's all irrelevant now, anyway. Tonight's episode proves you hit pay dirt with your remarks."

"Which brings us back to your safety. I don't want you here alone."

"I can take care of myself," she said curtly as she sauntered to the door.

Jarrod closed the distance between them in two seconds flat. "Why are you being so stubborn about this?"

She flicked off the light switch to escape from the furor in his eyes. "Look, you've as much as admitted you don't really believe Nate could do anything wrong. If you think I'm only being paranoid, why should you worry about me being here by myself?"

"I don't have to be completely convinced of anything to worry about you," he said earnestly. "What if you are right and Nate or someone else showed up again tonight? I'd never forgive myself for leaving you alone."

"I'll be all right." She was starting to close the barn doors when he grabbed her arm. The tension alone in his grip was enough to make her wince.

"What about the stallion? If you won't think about yourself, what about him?"

She glanced dubiously into the dark barn. "I doubt Nate would try anything else tonight."

"He might not want to waste much time. If he thinks you're on to him, he can't afford to sit idle too long."

"Maybe . . ."

"Let me stay here tonight."

She blinked up at him. "What?"

"It's the only logical thing to do. You can take the stallion out of here tomorrow. The rest of tonight is when he'll be in the most danger."

"Just where do you plan on sleeping?" she asked slowly.

His hesitation was brief. "Out here in the barn, of course. That's the best place to protect the horse, isn't it?"

"Yes." *If that was really why he wanted to stay.* It was more likely his true motive for sticking around was for a far different reason, but he did have a point about Ebony Fire being at risk tonight.

"So what do you say?"

"Are you sure you want to do this? I don't have a cot or anything."

"I can spread out a bale of straw and you can give me a couple of blankets. It's better if I'm not too comfortable anyway. That way I won't sleep as sound."

She stared at him for a long time in the dim moonlight. Why was she so reluctant to let him stay? His argument made good sense. Ebony Fire would be safe until she could get him somewhere else where Nate couldn't find him. So how come she wasn't jumping at Jarrod's offer?

It suddenly came to her in a staggering flash of realization. If Ebony Fire was in danger tonight, then Jarrod would be as well. She honestly couldn't say which worried her more.

"You can sleep out here on one condition," she said at last.

"What's that?"

"I sleep out here with you."

For the first time in as long as he could remember, Jarrod was at a loss for words. He had to try his vocal chords several times before he could get out one syllable. "Why?"

She shrugged. "Ebony Fire is my responsibility, not yours."

"That's not good enough."

"Well, if I stay out here, too, then I can make sure you don't sleep through someone coming into the barn."

"Sorry, try again."

"You win. The real reason is that I want your body," she said flippantly.

One eyebrow raised in a mixture of amusement and disappointment. "You could try that one again with a little more conviction."

"No, thanks. Once was enough."

He found her chin in the darkness and caressed it with his thumb. "I don't want to have to worry about you and that blasted horse tonight. You stay snug and safe in your own bed in the house."

Such a simple, gentle touch. Yet it sent currents of electric awareness through her that were strong enough to make her quiver. She had to wonder for the second time tonight if she'd asked for more than she could handle. "I'd be too worried to sleep in there alone," she murmured truthfully.

"About the stallion?"

"And about you," she admitted unsteadily.

"You'd be better off in your bedroom," he warned softly. "There might be other hazards in the barn for you tonight besides Nate."

"As I told you before, I can take care of myself."

"I'll just bet you can." Jarrod smiled to himself and slid the barn door open again. "I'll put down some straw if you want to go get some blankets and a pillow or two."

"Anything else, boss?"

"Maybe some coffee." He leaned against the door and watched her head toward the house. His eyes centered on the sensuous sway of her hips as her willowy legs carried her gracefully out of his sight. Parts of his anatomy melted while others tightened. He exhaled slowly and shook his head.

He had the definite feeling this was going to be one hell of a long night.

Eight

Cassie paused in the doorway of the barn, arms stretched to the maximum with her load of blankets, two pillows and a thermos of coffee. With uneasy skepticism, she eyed the one large pile of straw that was spread out in front of the stallion's stall. She crossed the distance quickly and dropped everything onto the golden yellow bedding. It was no simple feat to override the compelling urge she had to bolt back to the house.

"I've been having a nice little chat with Killer, here," Jarrod announced. "I told him he'd have to learn to accept my presence tonight or else he wasn't going to get a wink of sleep. So far he hasn't taken my word for it."

Cassie glanced in at the horse. He was still the picture of trepidation. "He'll probably be our best alarm if someone does come. By the way, how are we going to protect ourselves if there is an intruder?"

"I don't carry a gun with me if that's what you mean. I'm a vet, not a police officer. I suppose I could pull out a hypodermic needle if you think that would scare anybody."

"Very funny." She nodded in the direction of her neatly stacked bales of hay. "We could always keep that next to us."

Jarrod followed the direction of her gaze. "A pitchfork?"

"Sure. They're pretty deadly."

"How do you know? Have you ever used one on somebody?"

"No, but they're nasty weapons in the movies."

"If it'll make you feel better, I can bring it over here. I can't promise you I'd use it, though."

"What kind of guard are you?" she asked with mock huffiness.

He snorted. "An inexperienced one."

"Well, I think it's a good idea to be prepared. Maybe you can just wave it around and look menacing if you have to."

"Hopefully, we're both being too imaginative about this whole thing and a weapon is the last thing in the world we'll need tonight."

"Why don't you get it anyway," she said. "I'll spread out the blankets."

Jarrod was on his way back with the pitchfork when his step faltered as he watched her. He'd noticed her change in attire right away when she'd come back to the barn, but he hadn't wanted to dwell on it. He did now. She'd traded her short-skirted waitress uniform for a soft jade jogging suit that molded to her in all the right places. Could that woman put anything on her body that didn't make her look sexy?

He gripped the wooden handle hard. She hadn't come out here for a romp in the hay, he knew that. And there was something fragile growing between them that he didn't want to shatter by pushing when he shouldn't. Yet it took every last ounce of willpower not to rush over right this minute, throw her down on the blanket, strip off her clothes, and cover her sweet naked body with his own.

He'd only had the merest of glimpses so far as to the wonders of being intimate with her. Just a couple of brief touches that, while exquisite, had become a tormenting tease of what could be. Like being given one single potato chip.

He longed for the whole bowl.

Cassie watched him out of the corner of her eye while she tried to remain busy arranging the blankets. The hunger in his gaze made her knees go wobbly again. *This was a mistake.* They hadn't been alone out here more than five minutes and already she wanted to scream from the tension. They were too volatile together. She'd underestimated the attraction between them, but that certainly wasn't her fault. Never in her life had she faced feelings like this. She wanted to fight it, but had no idea how.

"Coffee?" she asked tremulously as he finally came close. "I couldn't carry two mugs so we'll have to share it out of the cap."

"Okay." Jarrod slipped out of his sports jacket and hung it over a vacant hook on the adjoining stall door. Unbuttoning his long sleeves, he rolled them up to his elbows. He took the cap of steaming coffee from her. "I hope this isn't Decaf. I may need a jolt of caffeine to stay awake tonight."

Cassie sat down with her back resting against the stall and covered herself with a blanket. "You're planning to stay up the whole night?"

"I think it's a good idea, don't you? It wouldn't do us a lot of good to both be sound asleep if someone came in."

"My barn door can't be opened without making some noise, and we do have Ebony Fire and the other horses to alert us to any strangers. Besides, I'm a light sleeper."

His gaze lingered on her face as he sat down beside her. "So, go to sleep," he told her softly. "You really shouldn't be out here, anyway."

"We've been through that already." She reached out to retrieve the thermos cap from him. "If you're going to stay up all night, I will, too."

"You don't need to do that."

"I want to." Did he really think she would be able to sleep with him sitting there watching her? She sipped at the hot coffee, wishing errantly that she'd tried to bring at least one mug out here with her. It was cozier than she'd thought sharing the single cap.

"Maybe we could take turns staying awake. I'd hate to see you go all night with no sleep."

"I'll be fine. It won't be the first time I've sat up through the night in this barn. Whenever a mare's close to foaling, I stay out here to make sure she delivers with no complications." Cassie handed him back the coffee. "I'll sleep tomorrow once Ebony Fire is safe. He's worth losing a night of sleep over."

"Have you given any thought to where you're going to take him?"

"A little. There's an old friend of my father's I figured I could call. He lives in a pretty remote area."

"I could keep him at my farm," Jarrod suggested slowly. "I doubt Nate would think to look for him there."

"You and my stallion alone on the same farm? Are you serious?"

"He'd get used to me eventually."

"If you didn't kill each other first," she said dryly.

"It was just a suggestion."

"And I appreciate the offer, but I'm going to have to pass."

"What makes you think he'll be any happier around this friend of your father's?"

"He's not a vet."

"Well," he said, his eyes boring into hers, "I might not be the most popular veterinarian in Kentucky, but I know I'm the luckiest."

"Why is that?"

"Because I'm the only one who has you for a client."

She broke away from his stare to focus her attention on the ceiling. Did he think she was that gullible? "Spare me the lines," she replied tightly.

"I was being sincere."

"Sure you were."

He shifted his position until he was squatted down directly in front of her. "Why is it so difficult for you to believe I enjoy being around you?"

Her eyes lowered involuntarily to meet his. The intensity she saw there dissolved her irritation. He wasn't kidding around. "I don't know. I—"

"Hell, I've wanted you since the first time I saw you. You knew it all along, didn't you?" His voice came out in something close to a growl. "You knew how wildly attracted I was to you then, didn't you? Just like you know now."

"I don't think now is a very good time to discuss it," she said in a rush. He had dropped forward to his knees and was leaning toward her ever so slowly. With her back against the solid door of the stall, she had nowhere to go. She wasn't sure if that was a blessing or a curse. "I mean, we're supposed to be watching for Nate or someone, and—"

"So kiss me with your eyes open," he mumbled as his lips brushed against hers.

It was the lightest of contact. His mouth gently sought her permission, her response, her involvement. It took Cassie all of three seconds to give him the answer. With a partially stifled moan, her hands came up to cradle his head as she pulled him closer. The pressure of his lips increased, creating a surge of boiling need within her.

Her body trembled in anticipation for his touch, but his hands were on either side of her, supporting his weight. Yet somehow she found herself losing her sitting position as she slowly slipped down until she was prone on the blanket. The stiff pieces of straw that poked through the blanket and her clothing were ignored as her senses came alive under his taut

body. Every inch of her in contact with him heated to a feverish level.

Quivering fingers became steady as she freely explored the
rounded muscles, the flat planes, and the firm ridges of his
torso through the fabric of his shirt. While his tongue plun-
dered and conquered her mouth, his hips moved into hers,
lightly enough not to be too blatant, but distinctively enough
to communicate his need. The unspoken message sent her
senses reeling even as her body responded with heated
tremors that shook her to the core. Through the grogginess
of passion, she realized how easy it would be to completely
lose herself in him. It was not a comforting thought.

She suddenly broke her mouth free and gripped his
shoulders, holding on in an attempt to gather some semblance of control over the loud demands of her body. Control. It was something she always strove valiantly to gain,
something she fought like a tiger against surrendering.
Feeling it drift away now, she was brought up short. Besides, she had a horse to watch over. How could she have let
something purely physical interfere with that?

Jarrod noticed the transformation in her, and barely
managed to suppress a groan of frustration. He'd been
trying to hold himself in check, hadn't let his hands wan-
der, hadn't let his lower body press strongly against her, despite how badly he ached to do just that. Some instinct had
warned him she'd pull back again, and the tight rein he'd
kept on himself had simply been a necessity if he expected
to survive the rest of the night. Unwelcomed, unwanted,
undeniably difficult, but imperative all the same.

"Jarrod," she gasped, turning her head slightly to the
side, "it isn't the right time or place for this."

"Yeah, I guess not." He wanted to ask when the right
time would come, but he didn't think he'd care for her answer.

Cassie took a deep breath, still battling to curb her surg-
ing emotions. "We're supposed to be protecting Ebony
Fire."

"You never forget about that horse for a minute, do you?"

One finger reached up to tenderly, but regretfully, trace the cleft in his chin. "He might very well be in danger. You know how much he means to me."

"Yes," he said. "I do." He moved a few feet away from her and stretched out, his legs crossed at the ankles. With a sigh, he propped a pillow behind his head. "Why don't you get some sleep."

"I already told you, I'd rather stay awake—"

"Cassie, if you expect me to remain a gentleman the rest of the night, you'll stay on your own side of the straw, you won't talk, you won't do anything except close your eyes and go to sleep. That way I'd feel like a complete heel for disturbing you."

She opened her mouth and then closed it immediately. There was no one to blame but herself for the empty space between them. That realization did nothing to ease the tight coil of desire inside her. How could Jarrod possibly think she could simply go to sleep?

"I don't know why we can't just sit here and talk," she muttered, shifting to her side with her back to him. She jerked a blanket over her body, more for a sense of security than for warmth. Her body was still heated to a boiling point.

"I thought we could do that before," he said thickly. "Look what happened."

"I'll make sure it doesn't happen again."

"I can't give you any guarantees tonight, not with our present circumstances being the way they are. If you really don't want the two of us to end up as one by morning, you'll do as I ask. And if you need any further inducement, think about how you would feel if Nate were to show up and we were caught, shall we say, in the act."

Cassie felt her face fill with color. Perhaps if she tried hard enough, she could go to sleep after all. If nothing else, she could certainly fake it.

"You'll stay awake if I don't?" she asked.

"The only way I could sleep right now is if someone hit me over the head with a two-by-four."

She closed her eyes with a smile. "If you don't stay awake, that could be a possibility."

"I'll keep that in mind. Good night."

"You'll wake me if you get tired?"

"Yes. Good night."

"All right, good night." With nothing left to say or do, she resigned herself to trying to sleep. An absolute impossibility, she told herself. Completely out of the question. There was simply no way...

The sound of a hoof banging on the stall door woke up Cassie with a start. She opened her eyes with a jolt, only to find herself face to face with Jarrod's chest. As consciousness slowly edged away sleepiness, she also became aware that she was nestled close to his side. One of his arms was wrapped around her shoulders, while one of hers was thrown over his stomach.

"Cassie?" Jarrod's voice was hushed but insistent. "Are you awake?"

"Uh, yes." She sat up and stared into his bloodshot eyes in amazement. "How did I end up like this?"

"You just rolled over during the night." He smiled as he pulled a piece of straw out of her tousled hair. "It was nice."

She shook her head. "I can't believe I fell asleep. Did you?"

"Not a wink." He stretched out the arm that had supported her head for the past few hours. The night had seemed unending until she'd unknowingly snuggled against him. Then it had passed much too quickly. "By the way, I thought you were a light sleeper."

"I am, usually. Did I miss something?"

He opened and closed his hand into fists in an effort to restore circulation to his numb fingers. "Only that stallion kicking the sides of his stall about every half hour. Then there was the constant snorting he did. I don't know how you could sleep through it all.''

"I don't either." She stood up, noticing the sunlight filtering in under the barn door. "What time is it?"

"Almost seven."

"You're kidding, right? I never sleep past six."

Jarrod got to his feet and picked up a blanket. "I never kid first thing in the morning."

"Boy, I guess I sure must've been . . ."

"Been what?" he prompted when she paused.

Comfortable, she thought to herself. "Tired," she said aloud with a grin.

"Right," he drawled. "Well, I'll tell you what. I'll help with your morning chores out here, and then you can make me breakfast. After that, I'm going to head home and catch a few hours of sleep."

"I can take care of the horses. Why don't you go up to the house and lie down on the couch for about an hour? By that time, I'll have finished up out here and I'll wake you when I get breakfast made."

"No, that's okay. I like my idea better."

She gave him a shove toward the barn door. "Go on. You really look beat. Now that I know Nate didn't try anything last night, I feel guilty having you stay here watching over Ebony Fire when it wasn't necessary. An hour nap will do you good."

He shook his head and tried to scowl at her. He was too tired to succeed. "Do you always get your own way, Miss Malone?"

"Always," she confirmed immediately. "Now go."

With a muffled curse under his breath, he finally turned to leave the barn. As she watched him amble outside, she was struck by how fluid his movements were for a man who had gone twenty-four hours without sleep. She knew by looking at him how exhausted he was, but he didn't show it in his smooth, unhurried walk.

A stirring of desire swept through her, surprising her with
its intensity. She couldn't dismiss its significance from lack
of sleep, either. Turning away with a groan of resignation,
she admitted the unthinkable to herself.

She was falling for Jarrod.

Falling? No, maybe a more accurate description would be
plummeting. It left her feeling guilty and more than a little
traitorous. How could she let herself be taken in by a man
who'd indirectly been responsible for her father's death? A
man who still, she was grudgingly certain, refused to believe Nathan Hall, and not her father, was the louse?

She still didn't have any answers by the time she walked
in the house. Kicking off her tennies at the door, she tip-
toed into the living room. Jarrod was sprawled out on the
couch, sound asleep. She smiled at the picture he made, his
face shadowed by a bristly day-old beard, his long body relaxed, his hair in boyish disarray for the first time since she'd
met him.

It would be awfully easy to get used to seeing him like that
every morning. That acknowledgment was enough to send
her scurrying past the sight of him and into the bathroom.
Breakfast could wait. She was in dire need of a refreshing
shower. A nice hot one had been on her mind a little while
ago; now, she thought she might have to turn the water
temperature down considerably.

Emerging from the bathroom a short time later, she hesitated in front of Jarrod. Sleep was more important than
food to him right now, she decided. She'd eat breakfast
alone and let him be. Besides, she didn't want to worry
about him falling asleep later while driving home. He could
just as easily catch up on his rest right where he was.

In the meantime, she had a horse to hide. After gulping
down a bowl of oatmeal, Cassie made a quick phone call.
Minutes later, she'd left a brief note for Jarrod in case he
woke up, loaded the stallion into her horse trailer, and was
whisking him off to what she prayed was a safer place to
stay.

* * *

The afternoon sun was streaming through the picture window when Jarrod woke up. Disoriented and bleary-eyed, it took him several minutes to figure out where he was and how he'd gotten there. As he sat up on the couch, his gaze fell on a piece of paper on the floor being held down by a stone horse statue. After rubbing his eyes a few times, he got up and retrieved the note. He read it twice before dropping it back to the floor.

So she'd left him here and snuck off with the stallion to some secret hiding place. That's what he called trust. What reason did she have to be suspicious of him? he wondered with a frown. Hell, maybe that was why she'd insisted on staying out in the barn with him last night. She'd been protecting the horse from *him*.

"Get hold of yourself, Fitzgerald," he grumbled at himself. He was being ridiculous. His brain wasn't totally awake and functioning properly yet. Coffee, that's what he needed.

He strolled into the kitchen and was promptly disappointed when there wasn't a coffeepot in sight. Inside the refrigerator, he located a can of diet cola. It would have to do.

As Jarrod drank down the last of the soda, he noticed Cassie's white cat watching him from the doorway. He tossed the empty can into a wastebasket and headed toward the cat. It continued to glare at him without budging.

"What are you staring at?" he asked the feline. "Don't *you* trust me either?" The cat flicked her long white tail back and forth in sharp twitches. "Do you think the mistress of the house would mind if I used her shower? I could sure use one right now. Never mind voicing your opinion, I can read it in your yellow eyes. She wouldn't mind a bit, right?"

The cat bounded away just as he reached the doorway. Jarrod grinned and walked back through the living room. He paused at the entrance of her bedroom, feeling somewhat uncomfortable exploring her house while she wasn't

there. Still, curiosity won out, and he let his gaze sweep over
the interior of the room.

Decorated in many shades of blue, the most striking fea-
ture was easily the beautiful quilt on her bed. Pictures of
horses running on beaches adorned the walls. The lady must
like the ocean, he mused. He would love to take her somewhere tropical and watch her stroll through the sand, the
surf spraying in her hair. Maybe they could even rent a
couple of horses, and race the waves that crashed into the
shore.

He swallowed hard, forcing himself out of the all too
pleasant reverie. Ducking quickly into the attached bathroom, he was inside the shower in record time. The steaming water cleansed his body, but did nothing to cleanse his
thoughts.

Jarrod had a towel wrapped around his waist when he
exited the bedroom. He was still pondering what clothes to
put on when he caught sight of Cassie sitting in the living
room. Her large violet eyes touched him everywhere, and his
skin prickled from the heat.

"You're awake," she said, a catch in her voice.

"You're back," he countered. "Did you get that stallion
tucked away somewhere safe?"

She nodded. "I hope so. George McCabe was one of my
father's closest friends. I know I can trust him, and he's very
good with horses."

So, Cassie hadn't been trying to withhold where she'd
taken the horse. Tension was expelled along with his bated
breath. "How did the stallion take to him?"

"He didn't react with instant hate like he did with you."
Cassie concentrated on keeping her attention solely on his
face. His near naked body, sprinkled with a dusting of
brown hair and droplets of water, had the disturbing power
to make her lose her train of thought. She cursed the fates
that had brought her home before he'd had the chance to
put on some clothes.

"Yeah, well, there's no accounting for some horses' taste."

Smiling, she stood up and turned toward the kitchen. "I'll make you something to eat while you get dressed."

"Cassie?"

She stopped but didn't look at him. She'd seen about all of his brawny virility that she could take and still behave seminormally. "What?"

"I've got a clean pair of coveralls out in my truck. Would you mind getting them for me? I'd rather wear them than put my other clothes on again."

"Okay. I'll be right back." When she returned with the coveralls, she tossed them at him from the living room and hurried into the kitchen. By the time he joined her, she had a roast beef sandwich and potato salad on the table for him.

"That looks great," he said as he walked into the room. "I feel like I haven't eaten in days."

His physique was no less alluring than it had been covered with only a towel. Her gaze followed the half-zipped coveralls that exposed a good portion of his muscular chest, on down lower to his narrow hips and taut thighs. The room suddenly started spinning as her imagination went wild picturing him with the zipper lowered several more inches. Watching him, she felt like she hadn't eaten in a lifetime.

"Do you want something to drink?" she asked with a squeak.

He took a hefty bite of the sandwich. "I'll take another can of diet soda."

"Another?"

"I had one when I first woke up. I'm surprised your white cat didn't report that to you already. She supervised every move I made."

Cassie took two cans of soda out of the refrigerator and handed him one. She opened the other can and sat down across from him. It was far from easy to keep her mind only on the important business at hand. "Jarrod, how am I ever

going to prove Nate guilty of insurance fraud before he finds
Ebony Fire?''

"We'll find a way.''

He'd said *we,* she thought with a trace of irritation. A part
of her still hoped Jarrod might actually believe in her theory, but an obnoxious little voice inside her kept throwing
in the doubts. *He's just humoring you,* it would say more
and more often. She struggled to continue to ignore it as best
she could.

"Do you know what happened to Finish First's body?''
she asked.

"The horse that died in Nate's stable? It was cremated
after the autopsy.''

She circled the top of the can with one finger and sighed.
"Another dead end. Nate covered himself well, didn't he?''

"All except the racehorse himself. That's our ace in the
hole, Cassie.''

"I know, but we still have to figure out why. Why did he
do it all?''

"Tell me about the night Ebony Fire died.''

"Supposedly died,'' she corrected.

"Whatever. Maybe you'll remember something that
might help.''

"There's really not much to the story. My father, as you
know, was responsible for Ebony Fire's care and feeding.
He'd fed him that night just like every other night. The same
grain, the same hay. He checked on him before going to bed
and everything was fine. The next morning, there was a dead
horse in the stall. The autopsy showed death by colic from
ingesting moldy hay. There were still several flakes of very
bad hay in the stall when they discovered the horse.''

Jarrod's brow furrowed as he chewed. "Your father, if
he'd have been careful, would never have fed moldy hay to
a horse,'' he continued for her. "So, he got the blame despite the fact that the hay should've been checked when it
was stored.''

"Exactly. Nate started the rumors about my father being drunk and careless that night." She squeezed the aluminum can until it crinkled. "He hadn't been drinking. He told me that, along with the fact that he'd checked Ebony Fire's feed that night just like he had every other night. Nate bales his own hay on his land, and neither my father nor I had ever once seen moldy hay on that farm."

"Evidently, you think someone switched horses and put bad hay in the stall that night."

Cassie grinned derisively. "That's just what I told Nate. Not that he'd switched horses, of course, but that someone else had murdered his stallion with planted moldy hay. I called him plenty of names for making my father be the fall guy for a reason I couldn't begin to fathom."

"But didn't you or your father look at the dead horse that morning? Surely one of you two should have been suspicious if the horse in the stall wasn't Ebony Fire. Both of you were so close to him."

"I heard the news as soon as I got up that day, but there was already quite an entourage around Ebony Fire's stall by then. I could only take a very brief glance at him anyway. It tore me apart to see him lifeless like that."

"What about your father?"

Her throat closed up with emotion. "There were only two times in my life that I saw my father cry. Once was at my mother's funeral. The other time was the morning he thought Ebony Fire died. He was too shook up to see straight that morning. Besides, who would have ever dreamed it wasn't Ebony Fire who was dead? There was a black Thoroughbred with a white star in that stall. It was perfectly natural to assume it could only be Ebony Fire. No one would want to stare at a bloated, dead horse long enough to notice anything out of the ordinary about him."

"I suppose that's logical."

"And now I know that Nate had to make it look like one of his stable hands was guilty of negligence to cover up for a murder of a different horse. What I still don't know is why.'' She sat back in the chair and crossed her arms over her chest. "I've always wondered how they got that horse to eat the moldy hay in the first place. Thoroughbreds are notoriously fussy eaters, and there aren't too many that would willingly eat enough bad feed to give them colic. Maybe we should try to get a copy of the autopsy and you could look it over again.''

"What good would that do?"

"I don't know. Maybe there's something there that would hint at foul play. I know it's a longshot, but it's worth a try.''

"If there was anything the least bit unusual on it, the insurance investigators would have caught it.''

"I suppose." She stood up and carried Jarrod's empty dishes to the sink. "Why would a man want to collect on an insurance policy for a multimillion-dollar stallion? A stallion that had the brightest possible future ahead of him at stud as well as at racing?''

Jarrod scratched his head. "Ebony Fire hadn't been injured. I'm sure one of us would've known that.''

"So, his value at racing must have been all right. But maybe his value at stud was the problem.''

"Wait a minute!'' He slammed his hand down on the wooden table. "Nate had me run a sperm count on Ebony Fire that fall after the racing season was over. He needed it in order to syndicate him.''

"And?

"And I remember it was extraordinarily low. Ebony Fire was almost sterile. He would have been damn near worthless as a sire. Nate was outraged.''

Cassie was a little outraged herself. "It took you all this time to remember something that important?''

"Well, I—''

"Never mind." She rushed to his side and grabbed his arm. "That's our motive! Once word got out that Ebony Fire couldn't stand at stud, his value would have dropped no matter how many races he won. Nate had to collect on the insurance policy before they found out Ebony Fire's worth wasn't what he'd insured him for. He made more money killing him off than if he'd have let him continue racing.''

''But why—''

''Nate must have gotten greedy and switched horses so he could sell off Ebony Fire as Finish First,'' she went on. ''I wouldn't be surprised if Pete Erickson knew all along what horse he really had. Nate would've made more money on the deal that way. Ebony Fire was the superior racehorse. And to think he would have gotten away with it all if Pete Erickson had taken better care of Ebony Fire.'' Her eyes narrowed bitterly. ''A horse worth so much, and yet that jerk abused him.''

''I'd say Ebony Fire would be a handful for most people,'' Jarrod pointed out. ''He's lucky he ended up back in the care of someone who could handle him the way he needs to be handled. Someone who could give him very special care and understanding.''

She tried to ignore the flare of intensity that appeared in his eyes. ''Jarrod, if you took a sperm sample from Ebony Fire now, would that show it was the same horse?''

''It wouldn't amount to irrefutable evidence all by itself, but it would help.'' His thumb reached out to lightly brush over her lips. He smiled as he felt her tremble. ''If Nate's really guilty, we'll get him, Cassie.''

''Yes,'' she whispered. Why was she finding it so difficult to attribute her sudden exhilaration solely to absolving her father's guilt? It was the most important thing in the world to her—it had been her primary goal for years. Yet she knew her rapid pulse and flushed body had nothing to do with the prospect of convicting Nathan Hall. Abruptly, she turned away and sat back down in her own chair.

Jarrod stared at her for a long time, fervently wishing he knew what was going on in her head. On the remote chance that she could be right about Nate, he had to consider where he'd be left once she didn't need his help in the case anymore. Sure, he'd still be her vet, but would that be all? Did he want more? His body unquestionably said yes, but his mind and his heart? What were their votes? Lord, he was having problems thinking straight right now. He could only hope it was due to sleep deprivation and nothing else.

"Cassie, I really should be getting home," he announced wearily.

"Would you have time tomorrow to go with me out to George's and get a sperm sample from Ebony Fire?"

"Now, that sounds like a fun thing to do on a Sunday."

"I know you're very busy during the week, and I don't want to wait until next weekend to do it. Please, Jarrod?"

She could ask him to rope a rampaging bull and he'd probably do it, he thought in amazement. "All right. I'll pick you up around noon."

"Great." She stood up with him and followed him to the front door. "Thanks for staying over and everything."

"Any time." He winked at her, levity disguising desire for a mere moment. "And I do mean any time."

The fire in his eyes sparked a blaze all the way down to her soul. "See you tomorrow, Doctor," she said with a shaky laugh.

As she closed the door after him, Cassie could only marvel at how much she was already looking forward to it.

Nine

"Nice little place," Jarrod remarked as he and Cassie pulled in to George McCabe's farm. Nestled amidst eighty acres of pasture and woods, the neatly kept up barn and house looked like something off a serene postcard. Both buildings were painted a pale shade of green, which made the surrounding bluegrass fields seem all the more plush. Only three horses were visible from the driveway, but Jarrod could imagine there used to be quite a few more when McCabe was in his prime.

"George still takes care of almost all the upkeep around here," Cassie told him. "He claims it keeps him young."

"It must keep him busy, too." They got out of the truck and headed toward the barn. Right before they reached it, a large, bald man stepped out of the house. The sun glinted off his bare head, but the agile way he moved belied his bulk and seventy-odd years of age.

"Hi, George," Cassie greeted the old man. "This is Jarrod Fitzgerald, my vet."

"Glad to meet you, young man," George said. "Did you come to look at that feisty stallion of Cassie's?"

"I can think of words other than feisty to describe that horse," Jarrod remarked with a laugh.

"I didn't get a chance to call you this morning, George," Cassie said. "We've solved another piece of the puzzle. Jarrod remembered Ebony Fire had a low sperm count, so he's going to check my horse today and compare the results to Ebony Fire's from three years ago."

George's gaze shifted from Cassie to Jarrod. "I wish you both luck. I'll be in the house if you need my help for anything. There's an old John Wayne western on that I'm right in the middle of. See you later."

"Bye." Cassie turned and led the way into the barn. "Ebony Fire's in the end stall down here."

"Let's hope this goes easier than the last time I had to deal with this guy," Jarrod muttered.

A half an hour later, with the stallion's sperm safely on ice in the back of his truck, Jarrod paused before getting in the front seat. His eyes wandered over the secluded countryside, and the tranquility of the area seemed to beckon to him. They'd already told George they were leaving, but for some reason, he was reluctant to do so just yet.

"George won't mind if we take a little walk on his land, will he?" Jarrod asked.

"Of course not." Cassie looked at him curiously. He'd been in an odd, restless mood all afternoon, and it was starting to make her a bit tense. "Why do you want to go for a walk?"

"Oh, I don't know. It's a beautiful day and it's a beautiful piece of land. We don't have to go for a walk if you don't want to, though."

"I don't mind." She took his hand and tugged him in the direction of a large group of trees. "Let's go this way. There's a small creek down here that's really pretty."

They walked in silence, but Jarrod kept his hand firmly and possessively entwined with hers. He couldn't have explained why he felt so unsettled at that moment even if he'd wanted to. Maybe it had something to do with the nearly sleepless night he'd had, despite being exhausted. He'd managed to get a few more hours sleep during the late afternoon yesterday, but that had been about it. All he'd been able to think of was Cassie. He'd felt slightly mollified since picking her up today, but some unidentifiable inner agitation was still keeping him on edge.

"See?" Cassie said, pulling her hand free and motioning around her. "Didn't I tell you it was pretty?"

They'd arrived at a tiny clearing, with only a bubbling brook and a circle of trees as their sole companions. He scarcely noticed. His eyes were riveted on her. "Yeah, it's very pretty here."

Cassie swallowed and perched on the edge of a large rock that sat half in the water. "Is something bothering you today?"

"You could say that." Jarrod crouched down by the creek and dipped his hand into the water. He lifted his fingers, watching the water drip off until it stopped. "I didn't sleep much last night."

"Because you were overtired?"

"Because I was overwrought." His eyes drifted up to pensively meet hers. "Because there was a particular black-haired vixen who refused to leave my mind. Because I was so knotted up with wanting her that I couldn't begin to sleep."

Her throat went dry and she had to clear it before she could speak. "I'm sorry."

"I don't want you to be sorry," he said roughly, turning and dropping to his knees so he was within inches of her. "I want you to feel the same way."

"I do," she admitted, her voice a mere whisper. Her hand shaking, she reached out to toy with the top of the zipper on his coveralls. The metal was cool and impersonal; the heat of his skin through his T-shirt was not.

His fingers closed over hers, then tightened slightly, imploring her to look at him. When she complied, he saw a wealth of passion in her eyes so rich that his own hand became unsteady. "Cassie?"

She had to try twice before the word came out. "What?"

"Make love with me, right here, right now."

"But George is—"

"George is in the middle of a movie. He's not about to come strolling way out here. We're all alone, just you and me."

"But—" His lips cut short her next protest. They skimmed the surface of hers, as breezily wayward as the gentle wind that blew through her hair. It was a tantalizing invitation that she couldn't begin to refuse. His mouth continued to tenderly torment hers, pressing harder for a heartbeat, only to fade back in a teasing retreat the next. The combination was maddeningly arousing.

He bent lower over her, steady pressure from his head causing her to slowly lie back against the rock. The contact from his lips become purposeful then, his tongue branding and claiming her mouth as his own. His hips had settled between her legs, and with a muffled moan, his loins pushed subtly against her. Gradually his weight became too much for her, as she became more and more uncomfortable with the unforgiving stone beneath her.

"Jarrod," she managed to get out at last.

His mouth hovered over hers as he searched her face. "Yeah?"

"I think this is what's known as being caught between a rock and a hard place." She smiled seductively. "We can't make love on this thing, unless you want to be on the bottom."

He grinned and eased away from her. "You see what you do to me? I wasn't even aware of exactly where we were."

"I wasn't either, at first." She sat up, only to find herself a second later hauled down on top of him on the grass.

His lips found their way to the sensitive hollow of her neck. "Is this better?"

"Much." Her fingers curled up to feather their way through his hair. She could feel his heart pounding, strongly and erratically, joining the wild cadence of her own. Her teeth discovered his ear lobe, and she nipped at it playfully. Hearing his sharp intake of breath spurred her on to plant a row of kisses along the column of his throat. Then she was gasping herself as his hands trailed down the length of her, pausing on their return journey to float over the sides of her breasts.

"It's time to switch positions," Jarrod ground out, rolling her to her back as he went with her. He raised himself slightly so his hands had free access to the mounds of flesh he ached to caress without barriers. His palm covered first one of her breasts, then the other, as he massaged her nipples to erect peaks. Unsatisfied with just that amount of contact, his hands worked at the buttons on her blouse until he'd yanked the material aside. The front clasp of her bra was quickly released, and he finally had an open view of her full, rounded breasts. His head dipped at once so his mouth could pay homage to her exquisite beauty. After stroking each budded nipple with his tongue, he traveled down to explore the smooth skin of her stomach.

Cassie jerked reflexively as hot desire flooded her bloodstream. A primitive yearning coiled up and tightened deep inside her. Her fingers moved of their own accord and lowered the zipper on Jarrod's coveralls to his waist. He wore a white T-shirt beneath it, but she could still feel the coarse hair of his chest through the cotton. With a fevered groan, she called out his name while her hands clutched at the fabric.

"Tell me what you want, Cassie," Jarrod murmured as his lips moved over every inch of her exposed upper body. "Tell me."

"You," she said urgently. "I want you."

Her ragged admission alone was almost enough to drive him over the edge. He yanked off his clothes, then he reached for Cassie and with languid care he helped her remove every stitch of clothing she had on.

Passion. Never had it taken hold of Cassie so intensely, so overpoweringly. It frightened her as much as it electrified her. When Jarrod's naked body molded against hers, every cell in her body crackled to life and demanded more. She already felt ready to burst from sheer pleasure. How much more could she possibly take? Evidently she was about to find out, as Jarrod's hands roamed seemingly everywhere at once, pausing at last to administer their magic on the ultrasensitive core between her thighs. He sent her higher than she could have ever imagined possible, accelerating up toward an apex she'd never known existed.

Jarrod struggled to hold on, to keep driving her to fulfillment, but the need to unite with her could no longer be denied. He wanted to be right with her when she soared to the limit. Repositioning himself, he quickly thrust inside her. Her warmth enveloped him and urged him deeper. She pulled him closer still, and their unique rhythm hastily intensified.

Time froze as rapture was brought to the ultimate crest. And then, all too soon, they were carried leisurely back to the real world.

Consumed and spent, Cassie snuggled more solidly into Jarrod's embrace. For a long time, she was content to trace patterns in the hair on his chest with her forefinger.

"You're so incredibly beautiful," Jarrod told her softly, lightly kissing her temple. "And so incredibly sexy. Give me about three more minutes and I'd love to ravage you all over again."

"Hmm. That long, huh?" she teased. A balmy gust of wind blew across her face, drying her perspiration-moistened brow. She closed her eyes briefly, enjoying the sensation. Paradise couldn't be any sweeter than this, she mused dreamily.

Except paradise lasted forever. This moment couldn't. Reality was already pushing its unwanted way into her consciousness. Cassie started to move away.

Jarrod's arm tightened at once, keeping her captive. "Where are you going?"

She glanced around anxiously. "Jarrod, this was wonderful—well, better than wonderful, but I'd really like to get dressed again. I don't want anyone to find us like this."

"Okay, okay." He released her but didn't attempt to rise. Instead, he crossed his arms behind his head and watched her. When she'd replaced her bra and panties, she paused to look down at him. "What are you doing?" she asked.

Flickers of interest danced in his eyes. "Just enjoying the scenery."

"You could put your clothes back on, too." Flustered at his undivided attention, her jeans went on awkwardly and she fumbled with the buttons on her blouse.

"I will in a minute. Right now I'm too busy memorizing." It didn't take much effort. Every delicate inch of her had already become eternally etched in his mind.

"Jarrod..."

With a grunt, he got to his feet. "You're a spoilsport, do you know that?"

Cassie tossed her hair out of the way and bent over the creek. Cupping her hand into the icy water, she filled her palm and drank eagerly. It was far better, she decided, to concentrate on her thirst instead of her renewed hunger for Jarrod. Seeing him so casually slipping on his clothes did crazy things to the pit of her stomach. She didn't look at him again until he'd joined her at the creek bed. Even then, she was struck by the intimacy of simply sipping water side by side.

She stood up and shook the excess droplets off her hand. "We'd better get going. George is probably wondering what happened to us if he noticed your truck is still here."

"I guess." Standing, he reached out and plucked a small twig from her hair.

Her fingers instinctively combed through her hair. "Are there more of those in here?"

"A few, but don't worry about it. I love the natural look." One arm circled her waist. "Come on, let's go."

Comfortable without words, they ambled back to the truck. Cassie sat next to him on the bench seat, her head resting on his shoulder while he drove. The rightness of it all left her utterly at peace, and she dropped off into a relaxed sleep. Before she knew it, she was opening her eyes to find them back at her own farm.

"Do you have plans for the rest of the day?" she asked. "I mean, do you want to come in or do you have something else to do today?"

His silvery gaze gleamed with renewed flames. "I've got a few hours to spare yet. What did you have in mind?"

"Oh, nothing special," she replied as nonchalantly as she could. She wondered if he could hear her racing pulse, for surely it would have given her away. It stunned her more than a little that she could want him again so soon.

Just as she was unlocking the front door, Cassie became aware of her phone ringing. She threw open the door and ran into the kitchen to answer it.

"Hello?"

"Cassie, is that you?"

"Yes, Stacey, it's me."

"Oh. You sounded strange. Did I catch you at a bad time?"

"No, it's okay. What's up?"

"I've got another horse for you. I know it's getting late, but I was wondering if I could bring it over right now."

She bit back a sigh. So much for any romantic ideas. "Sure, Stace. What's the lowdown on it?"

"Purebred Arabian gelding, I guess, since he's got a freeze brand on his neck. He's about eight years old."

"All right. See you soon." She hung up the phone and turned to Jarrod. "That was one of the humane officers. She's bringing over a horse."

"What kind?"

"Arab gelding." Her eyes widened suddenly. "Jarrod, that's it!"

"What's it?"

"Stacey said this horse had a freeze brand. You know, they do that with purebred and half Arabians. It's done with liquid nitrogen."

"So?"

"So, liquid nitrogen kills the hair and when it grows back in, it becomes permanently white where the brand was. Ebony Fire's back leg used to be black, but it's white now. I'll bet Nate used liquid nitrogen to give him a white hind sock. It's possible, isn't it?"

He shrugged. "I guess."

"My farrier had an awful time trimming that hind leg, too. Ebony Fire could be sensitive to having that foot handled if it'd been hurt in the past. Do you think you could tell by looking at his skin?"

With a grumbled curse, Jarrod crossed the room and grabbed her upper arms. He'd pinned her against the counter before she had the time to react. "I'll tell you what I think, woman."

Fire engulfed her body at the predatory look in his eyes. She had trouble finding her breath, let alone her voice. "What?"

"I think that someday when all of this is settled with Ebony Fire, it's going to be damn nice not to have him as a distraction anymore." His mouth lowered to nibble at her neck. "Every time things start to get interesting between us, you bring up that stallion. He's the only thing you think about."

"No, not the only thing," she told him haltingly. She angled her head to the side in order to expose more tingling flesh to his eager teeth and tongue. His hips pressed against hers, making her dizzy with delight. Her mind began drifting away amid delirious pleasure when the last possible thread of sanity snatched it back. She pushed tenuously at his chest. "Jarrod, Stacey's going to be here soon. We can't—"

"Yeah, I know." He buried his nose in her silky hair one last time before stepping backward.

She took a deep breath and smiled. "I hate to impose on you again on your day off, but could you stay long enough to take a look at this new horse?"

"Well, I could," he said thoughtfully, "but it will cost you extra since it is a Sunday."

"You don't charge me anything for your labor anyway, remember?"

"I wasn't talking about being compensated with money."

She sighed dramatically. "In that case, I'll wait until Monday."

"You're no fun at all." He waved her off. "Go get ready for your horse. I'll fix us a couple sandwiches and then I'll see you out in the barn."

"Thanks, Doc."

Jarrod watched her hurry away before he sank down on a kitchen chair. He was dead tired and yet he'd never felt more awake and alive. But he also recognized the stirrings of anxiousness, too. Cassie seemed more determined than ever to prove her stallion was Ebony Fire. He'd held the slim hope after they'd made love, that she'd see things in a different perspective, that tenderness would easy away vengefulness. Obviously, it wasn't going to work that way.

How much longer could he let this go on? Things were bound to blow up between them sooner or later. He couldn't very well pretend to believe her outlandish theory indefinitely.

With a rueful shake of his head, he realized he now almost wished he could do just that.

Ten

―――――

"**H**ow's my favorite guy coming along?" Cassie said cheerfully, patting a long black neck that was finally showing signs of sleekness.

"Are you talking to me or that ugly old stallion?"

Cassie turned to smile affectionately at George McCabe as he approached. She dropped a quick kiss on his cheek when he reached her side. "Why, George, of course I was talking to you. You'll always be my number one guy, you know that."

The old man grinned. "Cassandra, if I was forty years younger, I just might believe that silver tongue of yours. As it is, I think you've only got eyes for that good-looking young veterinarian who was out here with you earlier this week."

"He is a handsome devil, isn't he?" she replied with a sigh.

George shook his head and chuckled. "I never thought I'd live to see the day that a man would be more important to you than your horses."

"You still haven't lived that long," Cassie said flatly. It was bad enough that thoughts of Jarrod had stuck with her every minute of the day all week, but having George see right through her was downright irritating. "Has Ebony Fire been behaving himself?"

"He doesn't care much for me, but we're managing. I think he misses having you around."

"I miss him, too." She smoothed down the stallion's forelock, amazed he'd come to accept her enough that he didn't object to the attention. "The only thing that makes it easier is knowing he's in good hands with you."

"And safe, I hope."

"I'm counting on getting all this settled very soon. I don't like putting you in any danger, but I just didn't know where else to take him."

"Look here, Cassie, if I can help clear up an old wrong against your father, no amount of danger would keep me out of it. You did the right thing bringing him here."

"Maybe," she said, but she couldn't help feeling skeptical.

"Did your vet friend get a sperm count yet on that sample he took?"

Cassie nodded. "He phoned me with the results yesterday. It was very low, but it's not conclusive proof by itself."

"What about that hind leg?"

"There's some wrinkling of the skin under the white hair, so it is possible it was treated with liquid nitrogen, but again, who knows?" She let out an exasperated breath. "We've got so many things to go on, but they just don't seem to add up to enough. My gut feeling and some circumstantial evidence won't convict Nathan Hall."

George squeezed her shoulder reassuringly. "Don't worry, honey. Somehow, you'll set the record straight. Your father will be able to rest in peace before you know it."

"I suppose it's silly, really," she said, her voice breaking slightly. "I've spent so many years with my biggest goal being to make amends for a man who's dead. I mean, how much difference is it going to make to my dad now? I should just be moving on with my life and forgetting about the past."

"But you can't," George finished for her.

"You're right, I can't. Not as long as Nate's running around a free man, I can't." She gave the stallion one last pat before turning to leave the barn. "I'm almost out of ideas, George."

"Something else will come to you."

"I did call to get a copy of the fake Ebony Fire's autopsy." She smiled at him optimistically. "Maybe when that comes, it'll show something that will help."

The Country Club lounge was little more than half full when Jarrod walked in. Although he recognized several people, he took a seat by himself at the end of the long, marble-topped bar. It took a few minutes for his eyes to adjust to the dim atmosphere, enabling him to make out Cassie's slender form through the smoke-colored glass that separated the lounge from the dining room. The sight of her was enough to shoot his blood pressure up substantially.

He ordered a club soda and shifted his position on the cushioned bar stool. Was it possible to become addicted to a woman? he wondered idly. He sure couldn't seem to get his fill of Cassie. It hardly seemed conceivable they hadn't made love since that first afternoon, an agonizing six days ago. Not that it was from lack of wanting on his part, for she'd awakened a voracious hunger in him that he doubted would ever be quelled. But one interlude of shared passions had been enough to make him stop short and reevaluate a lot of things.

And what conclusions had he come to after nearly a week of self-examination? With a grim smirk, he had to admit he'd come up empty. He couldn't yet put a name to his feelings for Cassie, but he couldn't stay away from her either. Just to what point they would progress, he had no idea. He couldn't wait to have the dispute over her stallion out of the way, but at the same time he was worried what would happen when they no longer had that shared bond between them. What choice did he have except to keep hanging in there?

He sat back and watched her, enjoying for a moment being able to satisfy the need to see her without her knowing it. His relaxation period turned out to be all too brief. Cassie was in the process of turning away from a customer with a smile on her face when her gaze suddenly collided directly with his. The smile faded at first as surprise claimed her features, then reappeared with a special little twist added to one corner of her mouth. It was a smile Jarrod had come to recognize as being reserved solely for him, and every time he saw it he felt a glowing warmth take over his insides.

His eyes followed her unwaveringly as she strolled through the dining room and up to his side. She propped one elbow against the bar and reached to take a sip from his glass. Her tongue slipped out to lick away the excess soda from her lips. Such a simple, unconscious gesture, he mused, yet it was more than enough to make him feverish.

"What are you doing hiding in here?" she asked.

"I wasn't hiding."

"Oh, no?"

"No." He grinned innocently. "I was observing."

"Observing what?"

His voice dropped to a rough timbre. "I was observing a very sexy lady who I wish I was alone with right this minute."

"Really?" Cassie made a grand show of looking all around the room. "And just where would this lady be?"

He grabbed her around the waist and pulled her into his arms. "Do you want me to show you?"

She laughed and bent close to his ear. "I'd love it," she whispered teasingly, then wriggled free. "Later."

"How much later?"

"I get off at midnight."

Jarrod glanced at his watch and shrugged. It was a little after ten. "I'll wait."

"I've got to get back in the dining room. I'll see you later."

He raised his glass to her as she breezed past. "You'd better believe it."

The headlights from Jarrod's truck reflected brightly in Cassie's rearview mirror as she drove home from work. He was staying close behind her, almost as if he was trying to push her into driving faster. There was obviously only one thing on his mind tonight, and although she'd attempted not to dwell on it for the past two hours, it was hard not to now.

He'd practiced stern control around her the whole week, never taking his kisses too deep or his caresses too intimate. She'd accepted it even though she hadn't understood it. The fact that he'd come to terms with something enough to want to sleep with her again thrilled her more than she cared to admit. She'd ached for him every night with a longing that stung in its intensity. Certainly that was the least of her problems. The biggest predicament she faced now was dealing with what she felt was a betrayal to her father.

If there was any way Mike Malone could know that she and Jarrod were lovers, surely he'd be frowning down at her from heaven. Her conscience badgered at her constantly, but she was doing a fair job of dismissing it. The one thing she could no longer dismiss, however, was how deeply she'd fallen in love with Jarrod. If she'd had any doubts before, making love with him had certainly squelched them. If only she could squelch her guilt that completely. The love she felt for Jarrod was too strong, too consuming not to be able to overshadow her remorse to a large degree, but could it ever be totally conquered? She had her misgivings, but she also couldn't help but wonder where all this would get her when Jarrod had yet to breathe a word about love or commitment. Would she someday see the past finally soothed away, only to see Jarrod get bored with her and move on?

There were no easy answers for that one. As she stopped at the bottom of her driveway and collected her mail, Cassie pushed all the apprehensive thoughts firmly from her mind. Worrying about it all would not change what was destined to be, she thought as she continued on up to the house. She had to take each day one at a time, and go from there.

"It's a nice, warm night, isn't it?" Jarrod commented as he climbed out of his truck.

With her car door still open, Cassie glanced at the sky in appreciation of the thousands of flickering stars before he closed the distance between them. Stars were quickly replaced by Jarrod's smoldering gray eyes as his hand came up to cup her chin. His mouth slowly descended, his lips gently brushing hers with tantalizing tenderness. The feather-light contact made her throb more thoroughly than if his kiss had been provocative and demanding.

"Do you have any idea how gorgeous you are in the moonlight?" he murmured, his hand leaving her chin to tangle among the waves of her long black hair. He stepped closer until he'd trapped her body against the side of her car. Both hands moved to splay out on top of the cool sheet metal of the roof, while he molded the hard length of his body to her sweet softness. His lips covered hers again, enticingly and suggestively.

A moan of sheer need rumbled in her throat. "Jarrod, let's go inside," she pleaded breathlessly.

His loins pressed against her arched hips. "Inside sounds like the perfect place to be."

"I meant inside the house," she said.

"I know what you meant." His lower body thrust seductively into her pelvis again. "And you know what I meant."

She sighed, entwining her fingers behind his neck as she clung to him. "And I couldn't agree more."

"Come on," he said harshly, peeling their bodies away from the car. "We'd better get in your house before I lose what scant fragments remain of my control."

Cassie reached back into the car to retrieve her purse and the mail. They were already in the house, the mail tossed carelessly on the kitchen table, when a return address on one of the envelopes caught her eye. She paused on her way to the living room and returned to the table.

"I've been waiting for this," she said eagerly, snatching up the envelope.

Jarrod turned, smothering a groan of frustration. "You have to read your mail right *now?*"

She ripped open the flap and tore out the contents. Her eyes flew over the document inside before she hurried over to Jarrod. "This is the fake Ebony Fire's autopsy! It's just technical mumble jumble to me, but it'll all make sense to you. See if you can find anything suspicious in it."

Jarrod glanced down at the paper she was holding out to him. "I thought I told you I'd already read the autopsy back when Ebony Fire died."

"Back when Finish First died, you mean." She waved the document at him again. "You did tell me, but you weren't looking for anything incriminating then. It's different now that you know it was a deliberate killing."

"But I don't know that," Jarrod replied carefully.

Excitement ebbed away to be replaced by something much colder. "I do," she said, equally as steady as him. "Could you please just look at it?"

Jarrod's gaze never left her face as he slowly took the paper. Tension, challenge, and accusations permeated the air, but this time he knew he couldn't simply go along. Out of duty, and not out of interest, his eyes scanned the autopsy. He held it back out to her with a shrug.

"There's nothing out of the ordinary here," he told her flatly. "Death by colic from moldy hay. It's cut-and-dried."

Her eyes narrowed dangerously. "You didn't even read it."

"Cassie—"

"Look, Jarrod, don't patronize me. If you don't want to read it, fine. Just don't pretend you did and tell me otherwise."

"If I hadn't scrutinized Ebony Fire's autopsy before, I would now. But—"

"Finish First's autopsy!" she corrected hotly.

"No, it's Ebony Fire's autopsy!" He threw the paper on the floor and steadfastly grabbed her upper arms. "Ebony Fire is dead, Cassie. As much as you want it to be otherwise, you can't change what happened. Sooner or later, you're going to have to face up to that!"

Her voice shook with anger. "You've never believed it for a minute, have you? All this time, you never once thought my theory could be right, did you?"

"That's not the point here."

"Then what is the point?" With a strenuous jerk, she pulled free of his grasp. "I'll tell you the point, Jarrod. The point is, you decided to play this little game with me. You made believe you were helping me, when all along you weren't really helping me at all, were you? Why did you do it? To get close enough to me to get in my bed?"

"That's the most idiotic thing I've ever heard," he burst out.

"Is it? You told me you'd wanted to kiss me for years. I would guess that means you wanted to do a lot of other things as well."

"Of course I wanted to make love to you. You're the most beautiful, intriguing woman I've ever known."

"Who also just happens to be chasing rainbows?" she supplied indignantly.

"Who also just happens to want something so badly that she's grasping at straws," he corrected. "I did want to help you, Cassie. I still do. But I want to help you get over this bitterness, this vengefulness that's a part of you.''

She laughed scornfully. "By being dishonest and sleeping with me? Thanks all the same, but I could have used a lot more productive help than that.''

"If only you'd accept the facts—"

"Facts? You want facts? The fact is you have no idea what I've been through. Your father is alive and well, rich and happy. My father got framed and fired. He lost all his self-respect and self-worth. He drank to forget, until one miserable day he decided to forget forever by killing himself with alcohol. It hurt twice as bad for me because I knew he'd been innocent. And now I have the chance to see justice done, to prove to everyone that Nathan Hall should've gotten their scorn, not my father. I can do that just as easily without what you consider your help. That's another fact.''

Jarrod shook his head. "I wish I knew how to get through to you," he murmured gently.

She softened momentarily at his show of tenderness, then bristled immediately in vexation. She'd let herself be swayed by his suave charm too many times. There was no way she was going to make that mistake again. "Instead of trying to get through to me, why don't you just get out?''

"What?''

"I mean it. I want you to leave.''

He hesitated. "For how long?''

"Until the time comes you can trust my judgment and believe the stallion staying at George McCabe's is Ebony Fire.''

"Or until hell freezes over, whichever comes first, is that it?'' he asked dryly.

"If you want to take it that way.''

"I—'' His response was interrupted by the aggravating sound of his beeper. Jarrod reached for the device in annoyance and shut it off. Crossing to the phone without a word, he punched in the number for his answering machine. After listening to the description of an emergency at one of his newer clients' stable, he slammed down the receiver. "It looks like you're going to get your way, at least for now," he said curtly. "I've got to go."

Cassie crossed her arms over her chest. "Goodbye, Jarrod."

He was just about out of the room before he stopped and turned. "This isn't over between us, you know."

"Don't kid yourself."

He smiled slightly as he headed to the front door. "I'll call you tomorrow."

"Don't bother!" she yelled after him, but she didn't know if he heard. The door shut, triggering the release of tears that came out of nowhere. She was supposed to be livid, not despondent, she told herself fiercely. Still, she couldn't hold back the sobs, and she was forced to collapse on the couch in a heap of misery.

She'd seen this whole thing coming, hadn't she? So why wasn't she better prepared to handle it? Somehow simply thinking Jarrod didn't believe in her father's innocence had been far preferable to listening to him come right out and say it. She could hardly fool herself now with any romantic delusions, could she?

Despite Jarrod's parting comment, it really was over. She couldn't continue in a relationship with a man who had so little faith in her and her father, a man who'd sneakily worked his way into her bed, a man who couldn't admit he'd been wrong three years ago.

With a heavy sigh, Cassie rose and wiped away her tears. She turned off all the lights and roamed into the bedroom. The darkness was easier on her eyes, but did nothing to assuage her soul. Not knowing quite what else to do with herself, she stripped off her clothes and climbed into bed.

"Don't worry, Dad," she whispered into the black night. "I'll still get Nate for you. Only from now on, I'm on my own."

Eleven

─────

Sleep that night was simply out of the question. Cassie confirmed that several hours later when she was still lying on her back in bed, wide awake, legs crossed at the ankles, her toes tapping restlessly against the sheet. Glimpses of the morning sun skimmed around her windowshade, announcing a new day she found herself dreading. With a turbulent sigh, Cassie dragged herself out of bed.

Sometime today, she'd have another confrontation with Jarrod. She doubted there would be any getting around it. Her mind was still a wreck from their argument last night. How successful would she be battling with him after getting no sleep? She could always hope he'd choose not to talk to her for a while. Maybe he'd even give up on her altogether and she'd never see him again. With a hint of curiosity at why that prospect didn't make her very content, she went out to the barn to take care of her horses.

Cassie was making a feeble attempt to eat lunch when the phone rang. A sixth sense told her who was on the other line, and she sat there, shaking, until it reached the eighth ring. Almost in slow motion, she lifted the receiver.

"Yes?" she said coolly.

"Cassie? Uh, how are you?"

"I'm fine. What do you want?"

"I think there's a lot more that needs to be said."

"I think we've said plenty already, Jarrod."

"I'm coming over—"

"Don't waste your time. I won't let you in."

He snorted. "Want to bet?"

She didn't get the chance to respond. The dial tone had replaced his voice.

Rising on weak legs, Cassie carried the rest of her lunch to the sink and dumped it out. Then she simply stood by the picture window in her living room and waited.

It didn't take Jarrod long to get there. A glance at her clock told her fifteen minutes had passed, but at the moment time seemed frozen to her anyway. In what must have been mere seconds after his truck screeched to a stop, he was pounding on her front door.

"Open it, Cassie," he yelled. "You can't afford to pay for a new door if I break through this one."

He was right about that. Besides, the sooner this was over, the better. Expelling her pent-up breath, she went to the door and unlocked it. She'd no more than turned the bolt when the door was pushed open. Jarrod strode past her into the room.

"Come in," she invited tartly.

Jarrod's gaze hastily skimmed over every inch of her. Evidently the last twelve hours had done little to soften her viewpoint. She was the picture of rigid aloofness. Almost as an afterthought, he noticed the dark shadows under her eyes. "You look like you didn't sleep a wink last night."

He looked tired and off-balance, Cassie thought. She swallowed down the tide of sympathy and caring that flooded her, even now. *You have to forget about him,* she reminded herself. "I slept just fine," she lied. "What is it you want to say?"

One hand swept agitatedly through his hair. "Look, this is nothing we can't work out. I've thought a lot about it, and I'd really like to take a good look at that autopsy for you."

Her eyebrows arched in vague amusement. "Do you honestly think you can fix everything by simply indulging me about the autopsy?"

"I wouldn't be looking at it to indulge you." Restlessly, he paced the confines of the living room, pausing in front of the aquarium. "Anyway, I don't see why it makes that much of a difference whether or not I completely believe your horse is Ebony Fire. As long as you believe it, you should keep trying to prove it."

"Last night you said I should face the fact that Ebony Fire is dead."

"I guess as long as there's a remote chance you could be right, then you shouldn't give up."

Exhaustion suddenly hit her like a crashing wave. She sat down on the couch and rubbed her temples. "Why are you doing this?"

"Doing what?"

"This turnabout. It sounds to me like just another ploy to get what you want."

"Why can't you accept that I've had a change of heart?"

"I stopped believing in miracles a long time ago."

He turned away from the tank and stared instead into the fathomless depths of her sapphire eyes. "Cassie, I'm sorry about your father. Surely, you at least believe that."

"You should have been sorry three years ago when you got him fired."

Surprise made his voice falter. "I didn't get him fired. Why in the world would you think that?"

"I was there the day you got back from your conference," she informed him icily. "When you heard what happened to your precious champion patient, you blew up. You ranted and raved at Nate for half an hour. Are you going to deny that you recommended Nate get rid of an employee who'd been so careless?''

Jarrod walked over and sat down on the other end of the couch. "I didn't know you were in earshot that day."

"You wouldn't have cared if you had."

"Still, I've never had enough power over Nate to get him to do anything like that. He had it in his mind all along to fire your father. I just reinforced what he'd already decided."

"Maybe, maybe not." Her gaze swung to meet his squarely. "I think you won't give my theory a chance because you can't admit you were wrong. You looked at a handful of evidence three years ago and jumped to some hasty conclusions. I think your ego won't let you reconsider your presumption."

"And I still think you're reaching for something in this business with Ebony Fire that almost certainly isn't there."

"At least I don't have a closed mind."

"Really? I'd say it's locked tight."

Fury rumbled in her, deep and oppressive. "And I'd say you were a sly, calculating opportunist."

"Why? No, let me guess. We're back to us sleeping together again, aren't we?"

"You were deceitful in the way you seduced me and you know it." She laughed without an iota of humor. "It was very gallant of you to spend the night in my barn with me when you never really thought my stallion was in any danger. You must have been quite disappointed at the time after the night turned out like it did."

Jarrod reeled to his feet, his own ire ignited to the boiling point. "No, I'll tell you, Cassie. As long as I've known you, I've never once been disappointed in you. Not, that is, until last night and today." He spun around and headed for the door. "Damn it, you just believe whatever you want to. If our relationship was based on so little that you can think the worst about everything I ever did, then it was never worth anything to begin with."

He'd rendered her speechless for the time it took him to open the door and put one foot outside. "Have your secretary send me a final bill for the rest of the medicine and supplies I've used," she called. "I won't be needing you as a vet anymore."

Jarrod turned to give her a heated, meaningful look. "Sweetheart, someday you'll realize you need me for a hell of a lot more than that."

The door shut quietly behind him as he walked away.

Cassie stood pensively watching her stallion grazing in a grassy paddock, her arms crossed over the top rail of the corral. The jolting confrontation with Jarrod had left her numb and more confused than ever. She'd driven out to George's farm to be with the creature who was indirectly responsible for the whole mess. Observing him now, she wished she could find one-tenth the solace he seemed to have.

"I just don't know what to think anymore, George," she murmured to the man at her side. She'd told him about the argument with Jarrod, but he'd kept mostly silent throughout the discussion. "You don't think I'm living in a dreamworld believing that stallion is Ebony Fire, do you?"

"If you believe it, it's good enough for me."

"Why can't Jarrod feel that way? He thinks I'm crazy."

George shrugged. "I've never known that it was a prerequisite for a couple to agree about everything in order to keep on being a couple. In fact, if it was, I think there'd be a lot more single people in the world."

"But they should agree on the really important issues," she persisted.

"Cassie, in the long run, how important is this issue?"

"How can you ask that! You know how much it would mean to me to resurrect my father's reputation and see Nate get his due."

"Yeah, I know that," he said. "But I also know you can't let it take over your whole life and ruin it. How do you think

Mike would feel about that? I'm sure he'd think it far more important for his only daughter to find happiness with a man she loves."

Dropping her chin to rest on her crossed wrists, she sighed. "I guess I want it all. Maybe that's part of the problem."

"Jarrod told you he wanted to look at the autopsy again, didn't he?"

"Yes, but only to appease me."

"So, why not let him help you again? If you really care so much about proving your case, I should think you'd welcome any assistance, no matter what the motive behind it."

Cassie gnawed on her lower lip thoughtfully. "I don't know if I could do that. Besides, Jarrod might not be so willing to help me anymore after our fight today."

"You never know until you try," George pointed out.

"But what if he doesn't want me to try?"

"Then Jarrod is the biggest fool in the entire world." He patted her back. "Listen, honey, I've always known you to have great instincts, about horses and people. I doubt you'd have gotten involved with a man who wasn't honest and decent deep down."

"I'm not so sure about that. My judgment seems to be a little off-kilter lately."

"Well, mine isn't. And I like the boy."

Cassie reached out and buried herself in his hearty embrace. "So do I, George. It would be so much easier if I didn't, but I do."

"There's no reason you have to be suffering like this, young lady." He pushed her out to arm's length and gave her an encouraging smile. "Give him another chance," he urged. "It's the only way you'll ever get this settled."

Cassie returned home from George's just in time to do her evening chores. She'd already given grain to the first four horses in the barn when she reached her pregnant mare's stall. The cheery greeting died on her lips as she opened the stall door. The mare was down in the middle of the straw, grunting and rolling erratically in discomfort.

Her heart in her throat, Cassie ran to the phone in the tack room. She'd already dialed the first four digits of Jarrod's phone number before she caught herself. She hung up, shaking from head to toe. How could she call him after the rift they'd had earlier today?

The man was a good vet, she reminded herself. He knew this mare, and he was the closest vet around. What choice did she have?

She'd picked up the receiver and started to dial again when a new thought hit her. *What if he wouldn't come?* He had every right to refuse after all the things she'd said to him. With bated breath, she finished tapping out the number. It rang twice before his answering service picked it up. She explained the emergency and hung up to wait for them to call back and confirm Jarrod would come out.

In less than five minutes, the service returned her call. Jarrod would be there within the hour.

Cassie didn't know whether to feel relieved or disappointed. She hurried back to the mare's stall and discovered her condition unchanged. For the time being, there was nothing else for her to do, so she finished feeding the rest of the horses. Compelled to be with the hurting mare, she slipped inside the stall and tried to soothe her.

The noise of the horse's periodic thrashing drowned out the sound of Jarrod's truck. Cassie had no idea he'd arrived until she suddenly sensed his presence outside the stall. She glanced over her shoulder and met his stoic gaze. She stood up and nervously wiped her hands on the back of her jeans.

"I didn't think you'd come," she said softly.

"I didn't think you'd call me," he countered flatly.

Cassie looked down at the mare. "She acts like she's colicking. I was afraid for the foal."

"You don't think I'm too close-minded to treat her?"

"I know I have that coming, but can't we put it all aside for the moment? This is hard enough on me as it is."

Jarrod bit off his retort and eyed her intently. She did look like a complete wreck. How much of that was due to the mare and how much was due to him? he wondered. "Put a halter and lead rope on her so we can get her on her feet."

As he watched Cassie scramble to do as he asked, Jarrod tried to restore his professional mask. He couldn't have been more stunned when his answering service told him about the emergency at Cassie Malone's farm. Surprise had given way to mild hope. He didn't want to put too much meaning on Cassie's call, but he couldn't help but feel she wouldn't have asked him to come if she hadn't at least partially changed her mind about seeing him. Could he get her to admit as much?

Pushing their personal conflict out of his mind as Cassie returned with the halter and lead, he concentrated on doing what he did best. They were able to get the mare to stand, and he performed a quick examination.

"Cassie, I'm sorry," he murmured solemnly as he stripped off his surgical glove.

"About what?" she asked in a rush.

"The mare is going into premature labor. The foal is already dead."

Cassie wrapped her arms around the mare's neck and hugged her. Her voice came out a mere whisper. "She'll be all right, though, won't she?"

He nodded. "She should be, as long as everything evacuates her uterus cleanly. I'll stay here until it happens to make sure she doesn't have any trouble."

She felt the tears coming, and closed her eyes to ward them off. "Thanks."

"You can take off the lead rope now," he suggested gently. "It would be best if you'd wait outside the stall. I don't think this is going to take very long."

Cassie left the stall without a word. She closed the door behind her and sat down with her back against it. Death was not an easy thing for her to deal with, even when it was only an unborn foal. She realized her emotions and nerves were frayed right now, and that certainly didn't help. The only thing left for her to focus on was the hope that Jarrod could save the mare.

She had no idea how long she sat there, her brain in a fuzzy whirl, before Jarrod was sliding the stall door open. Leaning forward away from the door, she slowly peered up at him. He held out one hand. Without hesitation, she placed hers in it and was pulled to her feet.

"It's over," he told her, his facial features tight and strained. "The mare came through fine."

She stood there for an eternity, inches away from him, while tears pooled in her eyes and then streamed down her cheeks. She never noticed. Her attention was riveted on the single tear that dropped from one of Jarrod's penetrating gray eyes. Some inner sense guided her finger to reach up and touch the wetness.

"What..." All at once choked up, Cassie had to swallow and try again. "What is this for?"

His gaze left her face to stare in shock at her raised finger. "I—I'm not sure." He dried off his cheek with a brush of one sleeve. "I guess I feel bad for you, since I know how much you wanted that foal."

"Oh, Jarrod..."

It was then that it hit him. He'd crossed the line without even knowing it. He'd gotten involved with Cassie and her horses to the extent that he'd cried for her, for her loss. There was no going back now.

"Why don't you go up to the house and wait for me," he suggested. "I've got to clean up this stall, and then we can talk."

"Jarrod, I—"

"No," he interrupted firmly. "We'll talk in the house."

Cassie didn't have the strength left to argue. She went up to the house and set a pan of water on the stove for coffee. A watched pot might never boil, she thought to herself, but it gave her something to do to pass the time. Just as a few tiny bubbles were rising to the surface of the water, she heard the front door open. Jarrod walked into the kitchen looking like a different man without his coveralls. Dressed casually in jeans and a T-shirt, it was hard to imagine him as the veterinarian who'd just delivered a stillborn foal.

"Coffee?" she asked.

"Yeah, thanks." He sat down at the table and absently ran his finger over one of the scratches on the wooden surface. "You know, I did a lot of thinking all day."

"So did I." She put two cups of coffee on the table and took a seat across from him.

"I came to a couple of conclusions." He took a sip of the steaming coffee. "Want to hear them?"

"All right."

"Even though you said you weren't going to see me again?" he added lightly.

"You're here, aren't you?"

"Yes, but would I be if you hadn't had an emergency with one of your horses?"

"I don't really know. Would you have come without there being an emergency?"

"Well, I probably would've let you stew for a while, but I would have come eventually." He sat forward with his elbows resting on the table and stared into the coffee cup. "You see, I realized I was partly to blame for what happened this afternoon between us."

"Partly?"

"Partly," he repeated. "I shouldn't have led you to believe I agreed with your theory about Ebony Fire, although if you think about it, you'd realize I did express some doubt the whole time. In a way, you were right about me doing it to get closer to you, but there was certainly nothing underhanded about it. Anything that gave me an excuse to spend time with you was perfectly fine with me."

Her heartbeat quickened, but she couldn't let the physical pull rule over her mind. "I could have dealt better with this whole situation if you'd been honest from the beginning.''

"Do you really think so?" He took a sip of coffee. It could've been bleach for all the attention he paid it. "You were in no hurry to get involved with me when I first became your vet. You wouldn't even admit our dinner together was a date. How do you think you'd have reacted if I told you straight out that I wanted to see you as much as I could?''

"Okay, you've got a point," she admitted reluctantly. "But I'm still having a problem with the fact that you won't take my case against Nate seriously.''

"Well, I've done more thinking about that, too. Maybe my ego had been getting a bit in the way. Although there's an explanation for every piece of evidence you've come up with, not the least of which is mere coincidence, I decided you could almost just as easily be right as you could be wrong.''

She had to smile. "Somewhere buried in the middle of that spiel, did I detect a simple 'Cassie, I sort of believe you'?''

"I suppose if you listened closely enough, you could've heard that," he said grudgingly.

"That was painful for you, wasn't it?" she teased.

"Not nearly as painful as the last twenty hours have been.''

Her gaze tangled with his. "It was for me, too.''

He reached across the table for her hand. "You know, I really thought you'd stay mad at me longer than this. Or did I miss the news?''

"What news?''

"That hell froze over this afternoon.''

Cassie pulled her hand away and sat back in the chair. "It didn't need to. You just admitted you sort of believed my theory, remember?''

He laughed at the trace of indignation on her lovely face. "So I did. That brings me to the next topic. I'd like to see that autopsy report, if you still have it around."

She studied him a long time before speaking. "You're not just being condescending to me again, are you?"

"Absolutely not. Let me help you with this, Cassie. If you are right, I'd like nothing better than to see it all exposed. But, if we find irrefutable evidence to the contrary—"

"We won't," she cut in.

"If we do..." he went on insistently.

It wasn't hard to tell him what he wanted to hear, because she knew it would never happen. "Then I'll give it up and let it go," she finished for him.

Relief spread through him like warm sunshine. "Good. Now, get me that autopsy."

Cassie retrieved it from her den and laid it out on the table in front of him. "You promise you'll look objectively for something suspicious?"

"Stop doubting me and sit down. I can't concentrate with you staring over my shoulder."

She could only keep quiet for a few minutes. "Have you found anything yet?"

"I'm not sure. This takes a little time." He slowly read through the contents of the autopsy again, analyzing every word.

"Well?" Cassie burst out impatiently.

"Give me a chance, here." Jarrod's eyes caught on one sentence. He reread it carefully. "Wait a minute! There were some slight lacerations in one of the nasal passages along with traces of hemorrhaging."

"So?"

His finger ran over another sentence further down in the report. "Right here is the notation that there wasn't any fecal matter in the horse's large intestine. That's very strange."

"But what does it mean?"

"And judging by the blood level and the analysis of the stomach matter, I'd say there's way too much toxic mold present. Much more than a normal horse would consume, even if he'd been starved first."

"What?" she fairly screamed in frustration. "Jarrod, talk to me in English. What are you getting at?"

He looked up at her, stunned in spite of himself. "The absence of fecal matter in the large intestine leads me to believe the horse hadn't eaten in a while. Racehorses traditionally are given hay almost on a free-choice basis, so there should always be a steady supply of feces in the intestine. If the horse had been very hungry, he might have eaten enough moldy hay to give himself colic."

"What about the other things you were talking about?"

"It could be interpreted to mean Nate wasn't going to take any chances. The condition of the nasal passages indicate the horse had been tube fed recently. Usually, of course, that's only done to put worm medicine directly into the stomach. I rarely do that anymore, and I know I never did it to Ebony Fire. There's no reason Nate would have called in another vet to do that while I was gone, either."

"Meaning?"

"Meaning it appears Nate injected pure mold, probably along with water, into the horse's stomach through a tube down his nose."

"How horrible for Finish First," she murmured.

"It was a hell of a way to die. He must've gone through quite a bit of agony."

"But is all that proof enough to convict Nate?"

Jarrod leaned back in his chair and shrugged. "It's hard to say. A case could be made that it's circumstantial, just like all our other evidence."

"So we're back to where we started."

"Not exactly." His hand reached out to cover hers. He felt her tremble when his thumb started to make seductive circles against her palm. "I'd say we learned a lot today. That's certainly progress anyway you look at it."

His fiery touch was almost enough to make her forget all about horses and revenge. Almost. "What else is there left for us to find?" she asked bleakly.

"Actually, I do have an idea."

"You do?" She couldn't keep the incredulous tone from her voice. "You put your mind to this for an hour and you've already come up with something else?"

"You don't need to sound quite so amazed," he said lightly.

Cassie waited for Jarrod to continue, but he didn't appear eager to elaborate. "So what's your idea?" she finally ventured.

"I'd rather not say."

"Oh, no you don't," she retorted, pointing a forefinger at him. "It's my father and my stallion. Don't think you're going to get heroic on me now and leave me out of something."

"You've done a couple things on your own. Now it's my turn."

Her eyes narrowed warningly. "Come on, Jarrod. I want to know your idea."

He rose from the table and stretched his arms straight up in the air. "I can see I never should've opened my mouth. I only brought it up so you wouldn't feel so defeated." He stopped to yawn. "Did I mention how tired I am? I didn't sleep last night."

"Stop trying to change the subject."

"Cassie, my idea is a long shot and could be dangerous. You're better off left out of this one."

"This is my show," she protested. "It's been mine all along. I confided in you in the beginning because I thought you could help me. It's not your place to take over. It isn't fair."

"Maybe," he said. "But I'm trying to be careful."

Fuming, she jumped to her feet. "You never even thought I had a case until a few minutes ago. I don't think you're the most equipped person here to do any investigating by yourself."

"Just give it up," he told her adamantly. "I've made up my mind."

"Well, I think you'd better consider changing it."

"You're just going to have to trust me on this. I'm not about to risk having any harm come to you. If we're right, the men involved in this are ruthless and have a lot to lose if what they did is uncovered."

"What makes you think you're so invincible?" she sputtered. "You wouldn't even use a pitchfork as a weapon."

Jarrod grinned and shook his head. "You're never going to let me forget that, are you?"

"No, but I'd like to try to make you forget about keeping secrets from me."

"You'll be the first to know as soon as I find out anything."

"When will that be?"

"Tomorrow."

How could she wait that long? "What about tonight?"

Jarrod took one finger and trailed it down from her collarbone to the sensitive spot between her breasts, and on further, stopping when he felt the waistband of her jeans. "What did you have in mind?"

"That's not what I meant," she said, flustered at her body's quick, trembling response to his touch. "Besides, you said you were tired."

"Suddenly, I feel wide awake." He wrapped his arms around her and kissed her silky hair. "I hate to bring up last night, but I did have some rather provocative plans before you opened your mail. What do you say we pretend all of that never happened and start from there?"

"That's the best idea you've had all day." She tipped her head to reach the pulse point on his neck with her lips. The strong beat vibrated against her mouth, filling her with the echo of his very lifeline. Every other thought in her mind disappeared except for one—how very much she wanted him.

His hands drifted up and down her back, pausing at times to press her slender form into the hard ridges of his body. "It was only a matter of hours, but you have no idea how I missed you," he told her fervently. "I nearly went out of my mind wondering if I'd ever get to touch you again."

"I wanted to stay angry," she revealed haltingly while her body caught fire. "I wanted to think I could carry on just fine without you. I wanted to pretend I was better off alone."

"But?" he prompted.

"But I couldn't." Her arms slid from around his waist to creep up the front of his brawny chest. They moved further to either side of his neck, her thumbs toying with his earlobes. She stood on tiptoe so she could feather an airy kiss on his lips. "Jarrod?"

He smiled down into her passion-glazed eyes and felt his stomach drop like lead in response. "What?"

"Take me to bed."

He didn't give her a second to change her mind. Lifting her off her feet, he carried her into the bedroom. Jarrod slammed the door shut with his heel after they went through, closing off the world so only the two of them remained. When they reached the bed, he leisurely let go of her legs, reveling in the feel of her soft curves as she gradually slid down the length of him until she was standing again.

His mouth blanketed hers, his lips roaming and seeking, wild for one moment and searching to be tamed the next. He kissed her with ravaging sweetness, thoroughly encouraging every hungry reaction from her. She opened her mouth with a faint whimper, imploring him to take her further. His tongue surged inside, stroking urgently until he felt her knees give out and she drew him with her onto the bed.

Taking an excruciating amount of time, Jarrod worked her T-shirt free from her jeans and glided his fingers underneath it to skim over her swollen breasts. She arched into his hand, her nipples taut with arousal. He pushed aside her bra and caressed the smooth, satiny surface, toying with the pebble-hard peaks while she writhed beneath him. Sheer need drove him to suddenly rise and yank off her shirt and bra so his mouth could continue what his fingers had started.

As his tongue encircled the tips of her breasts, Cassie's hands massaged the bulky muscles of his shoulder. Pure lust engulfed her, overpowered her, and made her long for more. Their clothing became a strong irritant, a barrier that kept her from experiencing the exquisite sensation of naked skin to naked skin. She tugged at the bottom of his shirt until she had the hem and rolled it up over his chest, pausing when it uncovered the sprinkling of rough hair on his firm pectorals. Her palms coasted eagerly over every inch of his heated flesh, nearly getting singed in the process.

Jarrod lifted his head and took hold of his scrunched up T-shirt. In seconds, he'd tossed it to the floor.

"Don't stop there," Cassie told him hoarsely.

"Okay, I won't," he murmured as he reached for the snap on her jeans. She kicked off her shoes while he lowered the zipper. His hands slid under the denim and lace, and he took the fabric with him as he traced a sensual line down from her hips to her calves. He stripped off her socks and rejoined her on the bed.

Cassie twisted away. "I think you forgot something."

"What?"

She nodded at his lower body. "Your pants."

"I can't promise how long I can maintain my control if I take them off," he cautioned.

"I didn't ask for any promises." She smiled, slow and enticing.

Jarrod quickly relented, then stretched out on top of her, nestled between her long legs. Nuzzling her neck, a moan shuddered through him. He couldn't begin to fathom how one woman could feel so good. The first day he'd come to her farm, he'd known he was a goner. Hell, he'd known it three and a half years ago. He realized that now, but he never could have predicted how strong the need for her would become. It was as if his emotions had been laying dormant for years, waiting for the right moment to burst into full-fledged prominence. That moment had certainly come.

His hands continued to covet her, starting with a stroke of her chin, then down to knead her full breasts, and on to graze over the velvety skin of her belly before dropping lower still to caress the very nucleus of her. The answering groan she let out evaporated inside him as he covered her mouth with his. His tongue probed deeper in matching tempo with his fingers until he sensed she was near the edge. Close to the breaking point himself, he repositioned his body and urgently joined with her.

Barely able to breathe, Cassie tore her mouth away from his. Her legs wrapped around his thighs, bringing him further inside her. She clutched at his back, only to find it too slippery from a light layer of sweat, so she gripped his tight buttocks instead. His thrusts grew in intensity, taking her on a lofty, sublime flight to euphoria. She cried out with him as the world exploded in a dazzlement of stars and sensations.

"You're incredible," Jarrod told her a few minutes later, gently kissing the tip of her nose. "I could lie like this with you forever."

"I know what you mean." Her delirious bliss, however, was all too short-lived. Now that her body was spent, her mind shifted unconsciously back into gear. "Jarrod?"

He snuggled into the cradle of her throat. "Hmm?"

"About that idea you had..."

But it was too late. He'd already faded into a relaxed, peaceful sleep. With a sigh, Cassie let her own eyes drift shut. She'd have to get it out of him in the morning.

Twelve

Cassie awoke at dawn, warm and content. Flexing her body under the covers, she rolled over to gaze at the man who'd loved her far into the night.

The other side of the bed was empty.

She bolted upright, anxiety immediately knotting her stomach. Knowing without looking that Jarrod had already left the house, she jumped out of bed and into the shower. She was furious with him for leaving without revealing his plan for today, but she really wasn't surprised. The man could be damn stubborn when he wanted to be.

It wasn't until she was already dry and dressed that she identified what was actually the driving force of her restlessness. She wasn't merely upset with him for leaving her out of his scheme and making her sit around waiting. He'd said it could be dangerous, and she was worried sick about him.

She couldn't let him do this alone. Do *what* alone? she asked herself for the hundredth time. What did he think of that she'd missed? Whatever it was, it was going to take place today. She didn't have a lot of time to come up with an answer.

Since she did her best thinking while doing physical work, Cassie hurried outside to feed the horses and clean stalls. As she worked, she replayed their conversation from the night before in her mind, hoping to gather a clue from something he'd said.

Jarrod had spoken of his idea being risky. Nothing they'd done so far could be considered unsafe, except for maybe the time Jarrod had baited Nate about her black stallion. What could he be up to now that might be hazardous?

Cassie frowned, closing her eyes to concentrate on the other things he'd said. *The men involved here are ruthless and they have a lot to lose...* Her eyes popped open. Jarrod had said *men*. Throughout everything, they'd always referred only to Nate, yet Jarrod must have been including someone else in his thinking last night. But who?

Two wheelbarrows of manure later, it hit her.

"Pete Erickson!" she suddenly shouted triumphantly. Jarrod must be going to talk to Pete. Hadn't they once discussed the possibility of Pete being fully aware of the scam? Somehow, they'd never carried out the prospect of Pete's involvement any further. But if Pete would confess to save his own hide...

In her excitement over finally being able to nail Nathan Hall, Cassie almost forgot her concern for Jarrod's well-being. What was important now was intercepting Jarrod before he got to Pete. Realistically, she couldn't imagine what help she could be if Pete became menacing. She only knew she had to be at Jarrod's side to face it with him. Cassie raced to the house to change. A phone call to Stacey got her directions to the Erickson farm.

As she drove the sixty miles necessary to get there, she could only hope she'd make it in time.

After sitting two hours in her car, Cassie decided she could never be a cop. How the police had the patience to last through a stakeout was beyond her. Although she did have one other very troublesome thought that was partially responsible for making her fidgety.

What if she was wrong?

No, she couldn't be. She'd figured it out logically, and now she simply had to wait for Jarrod to show up. That would hardly be so nerve-racking if she only had some idea when it would be.

Ninety more minutes passed before she spotted a truck approaching in her rearview mirror that looked like Jarrod's. As the vehicle got closer, it slowed down near the driveway. It wasn't until Jarrod had just about started to turn in that Cassie could tell for sure it was him. She honked the horn and leapt out of her car. The passenger door was unlocked, and Cassie had yanked it open and slipped inside before Jarrod had a chance to react.

He stared at her incredulously, unable to believe his eyes. "What the hell are you doing here?" he asked at last.

"Pull over and park. I need to talk to you."

Jarrod coasted to a stop in front of her car. "Now, what is this all about? How did you know I was coming here?"

"I figured it out. I—"

"How?"

"Probably the same way you did. A confession from Pete would seal our case."

"Assuming he knows enough to confess anything."

"Right." She twisted her hands together nervously in her lap. "Anyway, I'm going in there with you."

"No way."

"Save your breath. I'm not going to budge on this one." She motioned toward the driveway. "Let's go."

Jarrod reached across her to open the passenger door. "I'll go when you get back in your own car."

"I'll just drive up there myself if I have to." She slammed the door shut again and smiled sweetly at him. "I thought it would look better if we showed up in one vehicle."

"I told you last night I wasn't about to let any harm come to you, and I meant it. You don't need to be involved in this one."

"That's my decision, and I've made it. If I don't go along, then you don't go either."

One eyebrow jutted upward. "And how would you stop me?"

"I'd find a way." Pursing her lips together, she crossed her arms defiantly over her chest. "Really, Jarrod, you're just delaying this. You might as well give in and forget it."

"I don't like this," he growled.

"Then let's just leave."

Jarrod glared at her long and hard before restarting the engine. "All right, you win. You can come along, but I'll do the talking."

She wasn't about to agree to that, so she kept silent while they cruised slowly up the drive. After traveling around a sweeping curve, the house and barns came into full view. Cassie hadn't expected to see much in the way of class at the Erickson farm, knowing Ebony Fire had been neglected and abused there, so she was hardly taken aback by the run-down, shabby appearance of the place. The large Victorian house had torn shutters, a broken window, and badly needed a coat of paint. Four huge barns loomed off behind the house, but they, too, had seen better days.

"This is just how I'd figured it would be," Cassie replied as Jarrod parked the truck.

"It looks like the perfect place for a man like Erickson, doesn't it?"

"It sure does, although with proper care, it could be quite a nice racing stable."

"Well, if he wants to keep it going in any condition, he'd better cooperate with us." Jarrod opened the door and stepped out on the asphalt pavement. "Come on. Let's get this over with."

Cassie joined him in front of the truck. "Do you have what you want to say all planned out?" she asked in a hushed voice.

He nodded absently as a young stable hand approached them. "We're looking for Pete Erickson," he announced loudly to the boy. "Do you know where we can find him?"

"Mr. Erickson is in the yearling barn right now. I'll go get him for you."

"Thanks." Jarrod shoved his hands in the pockets of his coveralls. "Remember, Cassie," he murmured when the boy was out of sight, "let me do the talking."

She offered him a smile, but it was quick to fade from her face. The stable hand appeared again out of the nearest barn with another man on his heels. Even from the distance of at least fifty yards, when Pete Erickson's eyes met hers, Cassie felt goosebumps rise on her flesh. She sensed the repugnant side of him so strongly that it was easy to see why her stallion had clashed with the man.

It took quite a bit of convincing to get her feet to step forward. "Hello," she said coolly, taking the initiative before Jarrod could exclude her. "Are you Peter Erickson?"

The other man's gaze swung from her to Jarrod and back to her again. "Yes, I am. What can I do for you?"

"I'm Cassie Malone. I work with the humane organization that confiscated a black Thoroughbred stallion from you recently. This is my veterinarian, Dr. Jarrod Fitzgerald."

"So?"

Cassie returned the older man's hostile stare with equal malevolence. "We—"

"Is there somewhere private we could speak to you, Erickson?" Jarrod interrupted sternly. "It's extremely urgent."

For a moment, he looked like he would refuse. With a jerk of his head, Pete indicated the yearling barn. "I have an office in there."

"Fine." Jarrod grabbed Cassie's arm as they moved to follow Pete. "That's letting me do the talking?" he grumbled into her ear.

"I never consented to that," she whispered flatly.

"At least let me start the conversation. You can jump in when I've said what I want to say."

"We'll see," she responded under her breath as Pete slammed the office door shut behind them. Apprehension crawled up her skin at the stifling sensation of being in a closed room with such a sordid man. Already only a foot away from Jarrod, she edged closer to him.

"What is it?" Erickson barked, lowering his lanky frame into the chair behind his cluttered desk.

"I'm sure you're a busy man," Jarrod said smoothly, "so I'll get right to the point. The stallion that was confiscated from you has the tattoo number of a Thoroughbred called Finish First. Is that correct?"

"Yeah, that's right. What of it?"

"Where did you get this horse?"

"From a stable in Maryland. Why?"

Jarrod shook his head with a smirk. "You didn't get that horse from Maryland, did you, Erickson? You got him from Nathan Hall."

Pete leaned slowly back in the chair. "I've never bought a horse from Nathan Hall. Where did you come up with that idea?"

"That stallion wasn't Finish First, was he? He was really Ebony Fire."

Pete's ruddy complexion paled considerably. "I don't know what you're talking about. Ebony Fire died years ago. It was big news."

Jarrod stepped forward and propped his hands on the edge of the desk. "You think that was big news? I'll bet the headlines telling of conspiracy to commit insurance fraud will be even bigger."

"Just what are you saying?"

"I'm saying we've got a horse with a tampered lip tattoo, a man-made hind sock, and a low sperm count that matches Ebony Fire's. We've got an autopsy that screams of foul play. We've even got the motive."

"And," Cassie spoke up, "we've got a sworn affidavit from Finish First's former owners saying the stallion confiscated from you is not Finish First."

Jarrod glanced at her, hoping his astonishment wasn't evident to Pete. "Yes, we've got everything we need to bring charges against the people responsible for faking Ebony Fire's death."

Pete shoved the chair backward and stood up, his face now an angry red. "You two get the hell out of here. I don't have time to listen to these ridiculous, slanderous accusations."

"You'd better listen," Jarrod ordered. "We're here to give you a break. The way we see it, you weren't the one to think up this whole thing. You weren't the one who was responsible for actually killing Finish First. You weren't the one who collected a few million bucks off Ebony Fire's insurance policy."

Pete's eyes narrowed. "So?"

"We don't want you, Erickson. We want Nathan Hall. If you cooperate, you'll most likely get off the hook."

"You're crazy," Pete scoffed. "You don't have anything on me. Now get out."

Cassie watched the beads of perspiration form on Pete's upper lip. He was trying to put on a brave show, but she could sense he had his doubts. "Listen to reason, Erickson," she said. "The humane organization already has a case filed against you for animal abuse and neglect. Those charges are only misdemeanors. Insurance fraud is a felony. Do you really want to risk losing your horse business and ending up in jail over this? No one's going to believe you weren't involved. If you sign a statement against Nate, you could end up in the clear."

"You're bluffing," Pete muttered.

"Did you ever see Ebony Fire race?" Cassie asked. "I did, and he was a champion through and through. Not only that, but he had a unique way of moving. There are films around of him, and also of Finish First. The stallion you used to have is getting stronger and healthier every day. He'll never be able to race again, but equine experts will still be able to identify him simply by the way he runs."

"If you really had such a strong case, the police would be here instead of you," Pete said forcefully. "I'm only going to tell you one more time to get the hell off my farm."

"Have it your way, Erickson," Jarrod said impassively. "Don't say we didn't give you a chance. Let's get out of here."

Jarrod directed the last statement at her, but Cassie didn't want to leave without getting what they'd come for. "Pete, if—"

"Come on," Jarrod cut in sharply, grabbing her arm. He turned back to Pete as he was ushering Cassie out the door. "You think about it, Erickson. The police investigating this won't be so easily persuaded to drop their questions."

Cassie held her tongue until they'd reached the sanctity of Jarrod's truck. The she turned on him immediately. "Why did you pull me out of there so quickly? If we'd kept pressuring him, I'm sure he would have confessed. He was obviously guilty. Don't tell me you didn't see that."

"Oh, I saw it all right." He threw her a reproachful glance. "I also saw a man who was cornered and about to explode. There's no telling what he would have done if we hadn't left when we did."

She dropped her head back against the padded headrest and released a frustrated sigh. "But he was close to giving in," she persisted. "He knows we have him."

"Remember me telling you I didn't want you along? If I hadn't had to worry about your safety, I would have stuck it out a while longer with him."

"Oh, so blame me for us not getting a confession!"

Jarrod pulled his truck to a stop next to Cassie's car and put his hand over her knee. "I'm not blaming you for anything. We'll still get them, but it might take a little longer. Anyway, I think we've done as much as we can do. It's time to take it to the police."

"Do you think we have enough to get them to take this case seriously?" she asked gloomily.

"I sincerely hope so. I'm not too comfortable having Nate and Pete running around free now that they both will know we're on to them."

A smile lit up her face. "I like the sound of that."

"What?"

"*We're* on to them. You finally believe it completely, don't you?"

"The autopsy helped, but Pete's reaction was certainly the icing on the cake." His eyes held a touch of regret. "I'm sorry I ever doubted you."

"It doesn't matter anymore." Exhilaration over everything that had occurred in the past twenty-four hours made her giddy. "It's only a matter of time before my father's name will be cleared. It hardly seems possible."

"You were pretty impressive back there." He started to laugh. "Where in the world did you come up with that bit about Finish First's owners?"

She grinned victoriously. "Pure inspiration. It sounded good, didn't it?"

"Yeah, but I was so caught off-guard by your little revelation, it was hard to cover up for my initial reaction."

"Well, I had a lot of time to think up things like that while I was waiting for you to show up here. Although I was just bluffing back there, I figure we can get Finish First's original owners involved if we have to."

"That still might be necessary. We haven't exactly got an open-and-shut case, although I think Erickson might crack under pressure from the police." Jarrod reached over to trail his fingers softly down her arm. "Before you know it, Nate will be getting his due."

Her gaze held his, as expectant as it was hesitant. "Jarrod, I'd really like to hear you say the words."

He thought he knew, but he asked anyway. "What words?"

"About my father."

A smile caught at one corner of his mouth. "I guess you've earned the right to hear them." He picked up her hand and tenderly kissed each fingertip, his eyes burning intently into hers. "I was wrong about your father. I'm sorry I unjustly accused him of negligence three years ago."

"Thank you." She paused reflectively for a moment. "Do you want to know what I think?"

"Probably not, but I'm sure you're going to tell me anyway."

"I think your conscience has been bothering you for years. I think deep down, after you had time to let everything sink in about Ebony Fire's supposed death, you did have your doubts about my father's carelessness long before I discovered the horse I had was Ebony Fire." She reached out and poked his bicep. "I think that guilt was the main reason why you wanted to be my vet."

His expression turned pensive as he considered her statement. "Do you now want to know what I think?"

"No, but go ahead."

"I think you're too smart for your own good."

She laughed. "That's okay, you big tough guy. You don't have to admit it out loud as long as you admit it to yourself."

"Hey, I don't mind admitting to some things." He heaved out a long breath. "I guess you're probably pretty much on target with what you said. There, do you feel better now?"

"I feel impossibly great."

Jarrod's hand moved to tease and tickle the exposed skin on her arm, while his thumb lightly grazed the surface of one of her breasts. "You certainly do."

Her breath caught as thousands of tiny pinpricks tingled throughout her body. Had it only been a matter of hours since they'd made love? It felt more like weeks. "Are you done with your rounds for today?"

"Yeah, why?"

"I thought maybe you'd like to come over and do some premature celebrating."

"Premature?"

"Well, Nate hasn't been convicted yet, so we'll have to save the true celebration until then."

"And in the meantime, we can practice. Hmm, what an intriguing idea." He leaned over and dropped a quick kiss on her mouth. "Of course, it will have to wait until we get back from the police station. We should get the authorities on this right away."

She closed her eyes briefly and reached for the door handle. "I'll follow you there."

"Okay," he said. "And I'll stop on the way home and pick up a bottle of champagne."

Home. It sounded so natural coming from his lips. Hours later, when Cassie was heading up her driveway, the word was still reverberating in her mind. Jarrod had yet to mention love or a future together, but it was never far from her thoughts anymore.

She hadn't been inside the house for ten minutes when she heard Jarrod's truck arrive. A shiver of longing overcame her as she listened to the front door shut, followed by the confident, fluid footsteps she could identify in her sleep. He strode into the living room with a lazy smile, revealing the dimples that never failed to lighten her soul.

"Pink champagne," he announced, holding up the bottle in his hand. "Where are the glasses?"

"I don't own any real champagne glasses." She pointed to two wine goblets she'd set out on the end table. "I hope those will do."

Jarrod pulled off the foil from the top of the bottle and popped the cork. "Anything that holds liquid will do. It's not the glasses that make the champagne, it's the company you have while you drink it."

"In that case," she said as he filled the two goblets, "this should be great champagne."

"I couldn't agree more." Jarrod left the bottle on the end table and carried the two glasses to the couch. He handed one to Cassie and sat down beside her. "To Ebony Fire," he toasted, clinking his glass against hers.

"To justice." She took a leisurely swallow of the champagne, savoring the taste as well as the moment.

"To things more productive than justice." Jarrod leaned toward her, his mouth pausing an inch above hers. He watched her eyes flick up to meet his, her pupils large and smoky, before he lowered his head the rest of the way. His lips roamed eagerly over hers until an inner urgency drove him to seek more. He met with zealous encouragement when his tongue darted into her mouth, exploring the sensitive cavern that still held the tang of champagne.

Searing heat coursed through Cassie's veins, bringing a fever only he could break. Her free hand encircled his neck and her fingers massaged the bulky muscles of his shoulder. The nearly full glass of champagne in her hand was forgotten until she felt some of the drink splash over the rim.

"I've got to get rid of this glass," she murmured, withdrawing her mouth reluctantly from his. As she set her champagne on an end table, her eyes paused on the clock next to the glass. It was nearly eight. "I had no idea it was so late. Jarrod, I really should go feed my horses."

"Now?"

She stood up and nodded. "You know they have to be fed on schedule, and it's already almost two hours later than usual."

"You and your horses," he said with a groan.

"I could say the same about you. At least mine don't interrupt me by beeper."

He could only laugh. "All right, you do have a point. Go get started with your chores and I'll come out and help you in a few minutes. I've got to make a couple of phone calls anyway."

She hurried outside before she could change her mind. If anyone could ever tempt her into forgetting all about her responsibilities, it was Jarrod. Her love for him was so compelling it still astounded her.

Cassie had given grain to three horses when she got the intuitive feeling that something was wrong. The horses seemed alert and uneasy. She was inside the fourth horse's stall when a clipped icy voice pierced the silence.

"I was just beginning to think you weren't going to show up."

She jumped, the can of grain slipping from her fingers and mixing in among the straw. *Nate!* Her skin crawled instinctively, and yet some quality in the voice didn't quite fit with Nathan Hall's. Whipping around, she found herself staring into eyes as cold and hard as an arctic wind, eyes that belonged to Pete Erickson.

"What are you doing in my barn?" she asked through clenched teeth.

"Looking for something. Something that used to belong to me."

Cassie's fingers balled up into fists. "And what might that be?"

"Don't bother giving me the innocent routine. Where's the stallion?"

"Ebony Fire?" she shot out.

His mouth curved up in a sinister smile. "It's rather ironic that you of all people would end up with him, don't you think?"

"I'd say it's more than ironic. I'd say it's rather poetic." Rage rose in her to almost blinding proportions, hampering her thought processes. Something wasn't quite right, but she couldn't think clearly enough to figure it out. "Wasn't Nate man enough to come here looking for Ebony Fire himself? He had to send you to do his dirty work?"

"I do my own dirty work. I always have. Now, where's the horse?"

"It doesn't matter anymore. The authorities know all about the insurance scam. You were stupid to risk coming out here. You just proved you're involved."

"You little fool," Pete mocked derisively. "You think you and your vet boyfriend have it all figured out, don't you?"

"Obviously, we do," she retorted.

"Obviously, you don't." Pete pushed the stall door open. "I don't have time to waste with your obstinacy. I'm going to ask you one last time. Where is he?"

She held her ground as Pete reached out and grabbed her wrist. He yanked her roughly out of the stall. "Let go of me!" she yelled, struggling to get free.

"You heard the lady, Erickson. Let her go."

Cassie's head spun around to see Jarrod standing in the doorway of the barn. Pete's grip on her wrist tightened.

"Fitzgerald," Pete drolled. "I should've known you'd be close by. A small mistake on my part that I didn't look for your truck. Not that it would have mattered much anyway."

Jarrod stepped forward. "Let her go," he repeated with deadly calm.

"I can't do that until she gives me a little information. Unless you want to tell me where Ebony Fire is being kept."

"Why don't you try to get it out of me instead of her?" Jarrod challenged.

"No, I've always been one who prefers the easiest route. I'll work on her."

Jarrod blinked suddenly as realization sank in. "It was you behind the whole scam, wasn't it?"

"I don't know what you're talking about."

"You owned Finish First and switched him with Ebony Fire so you could race him, didn't you? You had to kill the black stallion in Nate's barn so no one would realize he wasn't Ebony Fire. Nate didn't even know about it, did he?"

Pete's laugh was chilling. "You're close, Doc. Damn close." He twisted Cassie's arm behind her back, making her cry out. "Your girlfriend has a lovely arm, Fitzgerald. It would be a shame to break it. For the last time, tell me where the horse is!"

In a flurry of movement, Jarrod sprinted to the pile of hay and snatched up the pitchfork. Holding it pointed straight at Pete, he advanced toward them. "And I'm telling you for the last time, let Cassie go."

"Come off it. You're much too cultured to use a pitch-fork on me."

"I wouldn't count on that if I were you," Jarrod warned. "I'm in love with her and I'd be doing the world a big favor by getting rid of you. I'll do what I have to do."

"Her arm will be broken before you have a chance."

"Cassie's arm will heal," Jarrod pointed out. "You'll have a chest full of holes. And you just might bleed to death before I got around to calling an ambulance."

Cassie glanced from one man to the other in horror. How could they talk so matter-of-factly about breaking her arm? She wasn't about to stand by and wait to see which man won his bluff. With all the force she could muster, she slammed her heel into Pete's instep and lunged forward. Taken by surprise from the sudden pain, Pete's grip loosened for a fraction of a second. Cassie wrestled free and ran to Jarrod's side.

"Leave it to you to take care of matters yourself," he told her with a touch of amusement. His eyes left her to center on the stall behind Pete. With solid wood walls from the floor to the ceiling and closely-spaced metal bars on the upper part of the door, it appeared to be a safe place to store Pete for a while. "Why don't you just back yourself into that stall, Erickson? With Cassie out of the way now, I've got a real clear shot at you with this pitchfork if you think about trying anything else."

Cassie didn't think he'd comply. But after considering Jarrod's words, Pete walked backward into the stall he'd caught her in minutes before. Jarrod latched the door, but he didn't set down the pitchfork.

"Go call the police," Jarrod told her. As she scurried off to the tack room, he eyed the desperate man in the stall. "It's over for you, Erickson. Do you feel like talking now?"

"Go to hell," Pete muttered.

Jarrod didn't say anything else until Cassie had returned. He looked down at her pointedly. "I guess in a way, we were both right," he said loudly.

"What do you mean?"

"You were right about Ebony Fire and I was right about Nate. He didn't knowingly commit insurance fraud. Erickson cooked up the whole thing. Nate's totally innocent."

"Don't be so smug, Fitzgerald," Pete called out. "You still got it wrong."

Cassie looked in at the vile man responsible for so much heartache in her life. "So why don't you tell us how it all happened? You've got nothing to lose now."

"All right, I'll tell you. Not to appease your curiosity, but because I'm not about to go down alone." He leaned casually against the gelding he was sharing the stall with, but the horse shied away. "Horses have always loved me," he commented with dry sarcasm. "Especially that demon, Ebony Fire. I should've put a bullet in that horse a long time ago, but killing him was too good for him."

Cassie longed to snatch her gelding out of the stall so he wouldn't be next to that monster, but she restrained herself. "Just go on with your story."

Pete shrugged. "Nate and I go way back together. We were friends in high school and college, and we each went our own way after that. Both of us wanted to race horses, but we sort of took different approaches to it. Nate did it respectably for the most part, and I, well, I looked for the shortcuts. I did all right, made some money here and there, sometimes legitimately, sometimes not. But I was pretty shocked when Nate called me up one day out of the blue and said he had a proposition for me."

"Killing Ebony Fire?" Jarrod put in.

"Yeah. He'd just found out that the horse was almost sterile, and he'd been about to syndicate that stallion for millions. Of course, that left Ebony Fire worthless unless he could make money racing. The problem was, Nate had insured him for twenty million dollars, based on his value at stud. When the news came out that Ebony Fire wasn't worth that much, Nate would have been forced to lower the amount he was insured for. I guess twenty million bucks and a horse with a questionable racing future was enough incentive for Nate to consider killing him."

"So why the switch in horses?" Cassie asked.

Pete grinned viciously. "That's where I came in. Nate told me of his plan a couple of months in advance and asked my help in killing Ebony Fire. He gave me a down payment for my services, and I decided to put that money to good use."

Jarrod nodded. "So you bought Finish First."

"I sure did, Doc. It was a brilliant scheme, you have to admit. I spent a lot of hours looking for just the right horse to switch with Ebony Fire. I couldn't believe my luck when I found a black one with a tattoo number so close. It was almost too easy. I'd get Nate's payment for killing a horse, and I'd get Ebony Fire to run as Finish First and make a lot of money in purses."

"So Nate knew nothing about the switch?"

"No, Fitzgerald, he didn't, that is not until you opened up your big mouth to him a couple weeks ago. I guess you could say I double-crossed him, not that he didn't deserve it. He got twenty million for Ebony Fire, but he only paid me fifty thousand to do the killing." Pete shook his head vehemently. "Hardly a fair deal, would you say?"

Cassie ignored his question. "Did you use liquid nitrogen to give the real Ebony Fire a white hind sock?"

"You got that right, at least," Pete retorted haughtily. "I have an unlicensed vet I use from time to time for delicate matters of that nature. He also changed the tattoo numbers for me and prepared the mold solution that killed Finish

First. Funny thing, though, Ebony Fire hated that vet almost as much as he hated me. I guess he doesn't have much in the way of pain tolerance.''

From off in the distance, Cassie heard the wail of an approaching police siren. They couldn't get Pete off her farm soon enough to suit her. She wondered vaguely how difficult it would be to sterilize the stall Pete was in. Then her thoughts switched back to Pete's deception. ''Did Ebony Fire ever race for you?'' she asked.

Pete spat into the straw. ''No. During the time his back leg was recovering and the hair was growing in again, he became a menace. He was a beast to train, fighting everything I did with him. I'd just about get him in shape to race, and then he'd hurt himself during one of his battles with me. Finally, I just gave up on him, but I decided to show him who was really in charge in my barn. He didn't take too kindly to my lessons.''

''You filthy, disgusting—'' Cassie started, but her words were cut off as Jarrod dragged her from the front of the stall.

''Come on, let's get away from this guy.'' She was shaking from head to toe. Jarrod led her to the doorway of the barn, throwing the pitchfork back into the hay on the way. When they were out of Pete's earshot, he wrapped his arms around her and pulled her tightly against him. ''I think I lost ten years of my life watching Pete drag you out of that stall. If anything had happened to you, I don't know what I would have done.''

Her heartbeat increased to a breakneck pace and she trembled all over in his fervent embrace. Warmth soon replaced agitation. ''But, of course you showed up just in time to rescue me.''

''Pitchfork and all,'' he added.

She smiled up at him adoringly. ''My hero.''

He grunted. ''Some hero. You took care of yourself when the time came.''

"But I couldn't have done it without you." The police siren screamed louder, and she knew it was getting closer. Her mind tripped on the one thing she'd been forced to let slip by at the time. She couldn't let it lie another second. "By the way, in the heat of the moment, I don't know if I heard correctly what you said to Pete."

"Oh?" he said, feigning ignorance. "What did it sound like?"

"I'm not sure. It was the part right before you said the world would be a better place without him."

Jarrod tipped her head back and gently smoothed the hair away from her eyes. "You mean the part about being in love with you?"

"Yes, that was it."

"When I saw your life was in danger, I called myself a complete idiot for not telling you before." His lips met hers, searing with promise as well as passion. "I love you, Cassie. With every fiber in my being, I love you."

"You don't know how badly I wanted to hear those words," she said, clinging to him as a tide of emotion threatened to bring on the tears. "I love you, too, so very much."

"Do you think you could get used to being a veterinarian's wife?"

"Yes, I think I could manage." She laughed and gave him a playful squeeze. "Just think, I'll get all my vet services free for life."

"Ha! None of this free stuff, woman," he chided her. "I'll expect you to earn those services."

"And how will I go about that?" she asked mischievously.

Two squad cars turned into her driveway, their sirens nearly drowning out his words. "I'll tell you later." His eyes swept from her moist lips to her shining blue eyes. "Or rather, I'll show you," he amended, his voice gruff and sensuous.

The policemen arrived at last and shut off their sirens. "Give me a hint," she whispered.

So he kissed her again, with all the torrid desire of an ardor that would blaze for a lifetime.

* * * * *

Available now from

SILHOUETTE® Desire™

MAN OF
THE MONTH
1991

What's a hero? He's a man who's...

Handsome	Charming
Intelligent	Dangerous
Rugged	Enigmatic
Lovable	Adventurous
Tempting	Hot-blooded
Undoubtedly sexy	Irresistible

He's everything you want—and he's back! Twelve brand-new
MAN OF THE MONTH heroes from twelve of your favorite
authors...

NELSON'S BRAND by Diana Palmer	in January
OUTLAW by Elizabeth Lowell	in February
MCALLISTER'S LADY by Naomi Horton	in March
THE DRIFTER by Joyce Thies	in April
SWEET ON JESSIE by Jackie Merritt	in May
THE GOODBYE CHILD by Ann Major	in June

And that's just the beginning! So no matter what time of year,
no matter what season, there's a dynamite MAN OF THE
MONTH waiting for you... *only* in Silhouette Desire.

MOM91AR

AVAILABLE NOW FROM

⬤ SILHOUETTE

Desire™

Western Lovers

An exciting series by Elizabeth Lowell
Three fabulous love stories
Three sexy, tough, tantalizing heroes

In February,   *Man of the Month*
Tennessee Blackthorn in
OUTLAW ($2.50)

In March,   Cash McQueen in
GRANITE MAN ($2.75)

In April,   Nevada Blackthorn in
WARRIOR ($2.75)

WESTERN LOVERS—Men as tough and untamed
as the land they call home.

Only in *Silhouette Desire!*

To order books in the Western Lovers Series, send your name, address, zip or postal code,
along with a check or money order (please do not send cash) for the price as shown above,
plus 75¢ postage and handling ($1.00 in Canada), payable to Silhouette Reader Service to:

In the U.S.
3010 Walden Ave.,
P.O. Box 1396,
Buffalo, NY 14269-1396

In Canada
P.O. Box 609,
Fort Erie, Ontario
L2A 5X3

Please specify book title with your order.
Canadian residents add applicable federal and provincial taxes.

DOU-1AR

IT'S A CELEBRATION OF MOTHERHOOD!

Following the success of BIRDS, BEES and BABIES, we are proud to announce our second collection of Mother's Day stories.

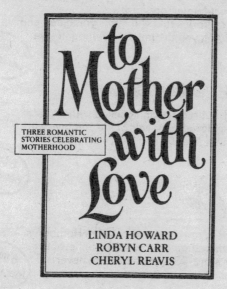

to **Mother** with **Love**

THREE ROMANTIC STORIES CELEBRATING MOTHERHOOD

LINDA HOWARD
ROBYN CARR
CHERYL REAVIS

Three stories in one volume, all by award-winning authors—stories especially selected to reflect the love all families share.

Available in May, TO MOTHER WITH LOVE is a perfect gift for yourself or a loved one to celebrate the joy of motherhood.

 *Silhouette Books*®

ML-1

FOUR UNIQUE SERIES
FOR EVERY WOMAN YOU ARE...

Silhouette Romance®

Love, at its most tender, provocative,
emotional... in stories that will make you laugh and
cry while bringing you the magic of falling in love.

6 titles per month

Silhouette Special Edition®

Sophisticated, substantial and packed with
emotion, these powerful novels of life and love will
capture your imagination and steal your heart.

6 titles per month

SILHOUETTE *Desire*®

Open the door to romance and passion. Humorous,
emotional, compelling—yet always a believable
and sensuous story—Silhouette Desire never
fails to deliver on the promise of love.

6 titles per month

SILHOUETTE·INTIMATE·MOMENTS®

Enter a world of excitement, of romance
heightened by suspense, adventure and the
passions every woman dreams of. Let us
sweep you away.

4 titles per month

SILG-1RRR

You'll flip . . . your pages won't!
Read paperbacks *hands-free* with

Book Mate • I

The perfect "mate" for all your romance paperbacks

Traveling • Vacationing • At Work • In Bed • Studying
• Cooking • Eating

Perfect size for
all standard
paperbacks,
this wonderful
invention
makes reading
a pure pleasure!
Ingenious
design holds
paperback
books OPEN
and FLAT so
even wind can't
ruffle pages –
leaves your
hands free to do
other things.
Reinforced,
wipe-clean vinyl-
covered holder flexes to let you
turn pages without undoing the
strap . . . supports paperbacks so
well, they have the strength of
hardcovers!

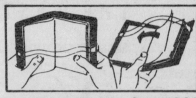

Pages turn WITHOUT
opening the strap

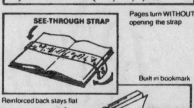

SEE-THROUGH STRAP

Reinforced back stays flat

Built in bookmark

BOOK MARK

BACK COVER
HOLDING STRIP

10˝ x 7¹/₈˝, opened
Snaps closed for easy carrying, too

Available now. Send your name, address, and zip code, along with a check or
money order for just $5.95 + .75¢ for delivery (for a total of $6.70) payable to
Reader Service to:

> Reader Service
> Bookmate Offer
> 3010 Walden Avenue
> P.O. Box 1396
> Buffalo, N.Y. 14269-1396

Offer not available in Canada
*New York residents add appropriate sales tax.

BM-GR

COMING SOON FROM SILHOUETTE BOOKS

ONCE MORE WITH FEELING

SONG OF THE WEST

by the BESTSELLING AUTHOR of
over SIXTY novels,

Two of your favorite love stories from an award-winning
author in one special collector's edition.

Don't miss the opportunity to relive the romance!

Available in May at your favorite retail outlet.

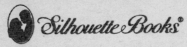

NR-1